"With compassion a Foster examines how family is pulled apart, not by the challenge of raising a young family far away from home, but by alcoholism. Leaving her husband in Tokyo and escaping back home to New Orleans with her children, thinking there is no other way but out, old friends show Lila that there is still hope if only she can learn to pray. Because when human strength is not enough, turning to God can make all the difference, as we find out in this touching account of one family's journey back to happiness.

"A compassionate read. Foster teaches us just how easy it is to pray. Even in our darkest moments, she shows how prayer can transcend human frailty and help turn our lives around. A book of hope and forgiveness.

"A must-read for anyone who has stopped believing in themselves or a loved-one. That with God's help we can overcome even life's hardest obstacles."

—Gretel Furner, Ph.D.

"A wonderful lesson. I love it. It's got to get out there."

—Lilly Pulitzer,
iconic clothes designer and author

"When Ricky tells Lila that alcoholism is a disease, not a disgrace, he introduces an element of hope into her life. With one in four families touched in some way by the disease of addiction, we know how critical it is to provide access to quality care and to bring hope into our patients' lives and the lives of their families. Jane Foster does a beautiful job of capturing the sense of hope that comes with recovery."

—Dr. Barbara Krantz,
Medical Director, Hanley Center

"Foster writes with compassion and depth offering the hope of God's love and grace for healing and wholeness through prayer. A must read for those whose lives are touched by the insidious power of addiction."

—Rev. Dr. Cecily Titcomb

The cover imagery is of Jackson Square, New Orleans (St. Louis Cathedral in the foreground and the French Market in the back ground).

Below Sea Level

Below Sea Level

JANE FOSTER

TATE PUBLISHING
AND **ENTERPRISES**, LLC

Published by Tate Publishing & Enterprises, LLC
127 E. Trade Center Terrace | Mustang, Oklahoma 73064 USA
1.888.361.9473 | www.tatepublishing.com

Tate Publishing is committed to excellence in the publishing industry. The company reflects the philosophy established by the founders, based on Psalm 68:11,
"The Lord gave the word and great was the company of those who published it."

Book design copyright © 2013 by Tate Publishing, LLC. All rights reserved.
Cover design by Joel Uber
Interior design by Caypeeline Casas

Published in the United States of America

ISBN: 978-1-62746-241-9
1. Fiction / Contemporary Women
2. Fiction / Christian / General
13.06.04

DEDICATION

To my darlings,

Giraud and Augusta

ACKNOWLEDGEMENTS

I love having this opportunity to thank my friends and family who read, listened, encouraged and made suggestions to Below Sea Level.

When I look at the list, I wonder what I did. There are so many of you who made a difference. I thank Kathy Snowden, Peyton Bruns, Anna Siwula, Billy Wister, Catharine Hamilton, Lorraine Odasso, Marianne Edwards, Dora Frost, Donna Casey, Chip James, Toinette Boalt, Susan Taylor, Florence Shinkle, Tommy Flagg, Chiqui Stahl, Lilly Rousseau, Lily O'Boyle, Dezia Restivo, Giraud Lorber, Augusta Lorber, Martin Lorber, Dawn Flynn, Carol Karman, Kate Winsett, Dawn Prossner, Kate Gibson, Annie Brown and Cecie Titcomb. And from Paris I give my special thanks to Gretel Furner, stellar professor of creative writing, and my writing group, the Breakfast Club, which meets on the rue de Varenne, and to my hostess in Paris, Bernadette Barbier, in whose beautiful apartment I wrote much of this book. I also thank my friends Sue Greig, Patricia Gastaud-Gallager, Christiane Fraise, Matt Jhonny and all the staff at La Rotonde who caffinated me during this process. I also want to thank my late English teacher, the great Lawrence Achilles.

God bless you all.

CHAPTER

1

The Louisiana summer heat was dancing on the cracked sidewalk. The song of the streetcar, the dilapidated palms, the din of weary cicadas tucked themselves around Lila and welcomed her home. It was a sweltering dog day in August. New Orleans stank of decay.

Lila was born here, four feet below sea level, twenty-nine hot summers ago. Driving up St. Charles Avenue toward St. Joseph's Children's Hospital, she concentrated on finding the new hospital, which had been built while she was living in Tokyo. Stopping at the light on Broadway, she looked around at the familiar scene and noticed the Katz and Bestoff drugstore was no longer on the corner where it had been all of her life. This drugstore was the citadel of social life for every Sacred Heart Academy schoolgirl. Now it was gone and without her permission. Sitting in the car, she thought of the jukebox, which had shaped her taste in music for life, and remembered sharing her secrets while eating French fries dunked in catsup and drinking cherry Cokes. She saw herself, Angie and Debo in green and white checked skirts, green blazers, and pristine white shirts. She saw them laughing. She saw them crying. Funny, she would not have thought of going in if it were still there, but now that it was gone, she longed for it to be exactly where it had always been.

The light turned green. Driving on, she felt the exhaustion of the past week set in; traveling from Tokyo with her four-and-a-half-year-old twins and the fourteen-hour time change were the least of it. Today, her only goal was to see Angie, but seeing Angie meant explaining. The very thought exhausted her. She took a deep breath and exhaled slowly, mindfully.

In the visitor's room at St. Joseph's, small toys were neatly placed in bins, large ones were at the edges of the room, their bright colors bouncing off the yellow walls. Lila sat there in a low plastic chair, her blond hair hanging limply around her face, shoulders hunched forward. She had not seen Angie in five years, but they had kept in touch by e-mail, the only one of her old friends with whom she had any regular contact. Angie had written to her about the accident and had chronicled her journey to becoming a pediatric surgeon, while Lila had shared her challenges as a new mother in a foreign culture and the day-to-day surprises of working for the *New York Times*. This correspondence was intimate, deepening their friendship.

"Look at *you*, mother of twins and teller of tales! You're a sight for sore eyes!" Lila and Angie hugged with that fierceness that comes with lifelong affection. Lila could feel months of tension slither out of her body.

"Oh, Angie, you have no idea how glad I am to see you! I was just thinking about the last time we saw each other. You were singing the blues at that dive on Canal Street wearing that red sequined dress. Now, look at you, immaculate in your lab coat. What a transformation."

Angie sat down on the orange sofa and patted the cushion next to her. "You just come sit by me, girl, and tell me every little thing! When do I get to meet Charlie and Charlotte?"

Twisting her hair up and sticking a pencil into it, Lila said, "Right now, they're at my parents'. Today, I need some time with you alone."

Angie rummaged around in a canvas bag. She found her strappy sandals and began to remove her sensible shoes. Sensing Lila's discomfort, she stood up, pulling Lila with her. "Let's go to the Camellia Grill. I'm starving." Angie stuffed the lab coat and rubber-soled shoes into the bag. Leaving the hospital arm in arm, they got into Lila's mother's blue Volvo.

They drove uptown in comfortable silence, savoring the physical proximity, each thinking of the life changes the last five years had brought. Lila had not told Angie about Philip who was no longer the funny, easygoing guy Angie remembered. She had not told her that the twins had been walking on eggshells from their very firsts steps. She thought how odd it was that she had left this out of what was otherwise an honest, almost daily report of her life in Tokyo.

At the Camellia Grill, they ordered rare hamburgers and chocolate malts. Lila felt comforted that the restaurant was still in the bright white clapboard building with dark green shutters. Four Doric columns held up the pediment above the porch, and the red brick walkway was bordered by a low white picket fence. They sat at the counter and twirled the stools so they faced each other. The windows were sparkling, and the summer sun streamed in. "I hope you are still singing," Lila said to Angie while struggling to suck the thick malt up through the narrow straw.

"I am, but to a different tune. After the accident, I just couldn't sing at the Owl anymore. I always knew my talent was second rate, at best. But I loved it for a while." Angie's pretty face was full of sadness. "Maybe I loved it just to shock my family. Quitting med school to belt out the blues was not what any of them expected, and you know, I always liked to keep them guessing, even Claude. Especially Claude, suited-up law review guy that he was. Of course, the accident changed everything."

"I wish I could have been here for you."

"You were in Tokyo with three-day-old twins, remember? No way you could have come. Anyway, I had all four of my grandparents, Aunt May, and Claude's parents too." Angie had written to Lila about her grief, saying it had a rhythm of its own, like the tide, coming in and going out, but always there, pounding. Pounding her soul into sand. Angie was looking out of the window at nothing in particular as if to divorce herself from the remembered sorrow.

"One day," Angie said, "a couple of months after the accident, Debo called and said there would be an alumnae retreat at the convent and asked me to go with her. I reminded her that I'm a Baptist. She said, 'God doesn't give a damn. He just wants you to have a break from your family.' I went with her. It was just right. Four days surrounded by loving, silent people. Mother Fitzpatrick told me just before we started the silence that grief honors love and that love never ever dies. I thought about this in the silence. The awful ache lasted a year, but I started to heal on that retreat."

"I can't imagine Debo on retreat. How did she make it without smoking?"

"She smoked in the garden. People weren't as neurotic about smoking then."

"Is she still working at NASA?" Lila remembered the pencil and pulled it out. A curtain of blond hair fell to her shoulders.

"Oh my God! Didn't I tell you? Debo is a novice at the convent."

"Hang on a minute here. Deborah Whitney Reeve is a nun?"

"Well, she hasn't taken her final vows, but she's a year on the way."

"What's she doing with all that MIT education?"

"Teaching math and science to grades five through eight."

"You've got to be kidding me." Lila arched her back and looked up at the ceiling for a moment.

Angie was smiling now. "Debo loves teaching. She says you have to get those girls before their brains get clogged with estrogen."

"What made her do it?"

"Just before she went into the convent, I asked her that. She puffed on her cigarette and said, 'There're enough astronomers, not enough nuns.' She didn't go on, but I'm sure she'll tell you. I was just too stunned to ask more at the time, and now it's too late. I see how much she loves her work."

"Debo, a nun? The last person I would ever expect." Lila shook her head in disbelief. "What do her parents think?"

"Her parents are surprising people. Living in splendor on First Street, kings and queens of Mardi Gras, you might think they just drink mint juleps and listen to opera, but not so. Before the accident, Debo sang with me a couple of times at the Owl. She's not a bad singer. One night, her parents came and acted like they'd never heard such talent. My guess is they love anything she does, and the only surprise is that she quit smoking."

"What about her brother?" Lila tried to sound casual.

"Oh, Bobby has an art gallery in the French Quarter on Royal Street. He sells nineteenth and twentieth century Louisiana art. Twice a year, there's an exhibition for a living artist. He's having an opening tomorrow night. We can go if you want to."

"Let's go. You know, I always had a crush on Bobby. Every time I went to Debo's, I would make a wish on the way over. It was always the same wish. That Bobby would kiss me, but he never did."

"Well, he's still a bachelor. Maybe he's just waiting for you, girl. In case you're thinking of dumping Philip." Angie arched her left eyebrow.

Lila's color heightened. "What makes you say that?"

"I can read between the lines." Angie shrugged.

"I left him on Monday. A week ago today. Last Sunday, he was on a cocaine bender, screaming at Charlie to get off the desk chair. He kicked the chair hard and sent Charlie sprawling. He got a great, whopping black eye. I couldn't send him to nursery school like that. So I kept both twins home. Philip came back around noon reeking of gin, rambling on about his childhood and who should be blamed for what. Suddenly, he noticed Charlie and said, 'What happened to you, kid?' He didn't even remember.

"I just stood there and said, 'I'm leaving Tokyo with the twins.' Then, Philip looked at me, seething with anger. He stormed out of the house, saying, 'Don't let me stop you.'

"I had to get out of there. So I called Mother and Daddy and said we were coming home as soon as possible, packed up a few things, and went to the Okura Hotel. The hotel doctor said we should wait a couple of days before flying to make sure Charlie's eye was healing properly. He could've lost his eyesight." Lila finished off her malt. "I don't know what's next, but I have an appointment with Ricky Wheeler tomorrow to discuss divorce. I haven't heard a word from Philip." Lila's mouth turned down. Angie was afraid she might cry.

"You made the right decision to come home, Lila. You can be sure that since the accident, I don't have any patience with drunks. But things will sort themselves out one way or the other, and I'll support you in whatever you decide to do. Ricky is a good man to talk to."

"I know, and he has been a good friend to both Philip and me. Right now, this very minute,

I'm so tired that I'm not sure how I'll be able to explain things to him with any coherence."

"You'll be fine. Just get to bed early tonight."

"Oh, I can get to bed early, all right. It's just getting to sleep that's the problem."

"I have some melatonin in my locker at the hospital. Drop me off there, and I'll get it for you. Tomorrow night, I'll pick you up to go to Bobby's opening at seven. By the way, in case I didn't tell you, I am so glad you're home."

CHAPTER

2

The twins were down for the night, happily exhausted from a day of being spoiled by their grandparents. Lila dressed carefully for the opening at Bobby's gallery. Alluring, not too sexy, that is how she wanted to look. Spraying the rose perfume, she made sure to put some in her purse, just in case she stayed out late. Her mother called to her, "Come and give me a kiss before you go out!"

Going into her parents' room, Lila noticed it had been redone during her absence. The all-beige room was now all peach, but everything else was the same. She had forgotten how heavy Louisiana furniture was, and even though the massive armoire, ornate desk, and huge mahogany four-poster bed were in the right proportion for the high-ceilinged room, the furniture made its presence felt with a personality of its own, a stabilizing influence for the house and its owners. The bed even had steps on either side of it, necessary mounting blocks, as the mattress was three and a half feet off of the floor.

Mrs. Parker was sitting on a shell-shaped chair reading a novel by Anne Rice. She had loved all the vampire books but preferred the new ones, full of wisdom, not just entertainment. She looked up from her book and said, "Wow! You look fantastic! Where'd you get those crazy shoes?"

"Hong Kong. They've got the best stuff there." Lila leaned over and kissed her mother on the forehead. "Thank you, Mother, for reading to Charlie and Charlotte and for making us all feel so loved."

"You *are* so loved, and reading aloud is my specialty! You and Augusta used to fight over what we would read, but once that was settled, neither of you moved a muscle for an hour." Smiling up at her daughter, Mrs. Parker removed her reading glasses.

"Remember when Debo used to come to spend the night? She always brought a Jules Verne book with her in case our reading was too lowbrow. My favorite was *Around the World in Eighty Days.*"

"I loved that too, and Debo was always one of my favorites. Is it true she's joined the Convent of the Sacred Heart?"

"Angie said she's a novice. I'm not exactly sure what that means, and I'm not sure Angie knows either. We were the only two non-Catholics in our class. But whatever it means, she has been at it for a year now and is teaching math and science to grades five through eight."

"Imagine giving up working at NASA to teach elementary school." Mrs. Parker gave her shoulders a little shrug.

"I'm going over to the convent to see her tomorrow."

"Well, give her my love and Angie too! You girls have a good time tonight!" Mrs. Parker put her glasses back on and continued reading, but she wasn't concentrating on the book now. Her mind's eye was watching Lila, Debo, and Angie grow up. She closed the book. Suddenly, she felt lonely, missing the children these women once were.

Hoping to meet the twins, Angie arrived five minutes early, but Lila said to forget it as they would never go back to sleep. The two women drove downtown in Angie's red Chrysler Sebring, top up, AC on. "Now, don't you go making any wishes tonight, Lila."

"Oh, I was only joking about Bobby. Anyway, it was a long time ago."

"Not to change the subject, but tell me what Ricky Wheeler said."

"He told me to think about this marriage seriously for a couple of decades before doing anything rash."

"Did you tell him everything?" Angie was grasping the steering wheel with both hands, peering into the blue dusk. Headlights were on in most cars, but not all.

"Just about. He says alcoholism is a disease, not a disgrace. He says that Philip was born to drink. Remember, his mother died of cirrhosis when he was twelve, and there're generations of drunks on both sides of his family." Lila adjusted the air conditioning and continued, "Ricky asked with a family like that what did I expect? I told him I expected an adult husband, responsible for his own actions. He just laughed and said I needed to learn more before I go and divorce a perfectly good husband. I suppose in some ways he's right, but Ricky should try living with Philip for a while. He wouldn't be laughing then."

"He has a point. Maybe you could get him rehabbed."

"I'm too mad at him to even think. Let's talk about somebody else, like Bobby."

"Girl, you just watch your step."

Bobby Reeve's gallery was in a nineteenth century building with a wrought-iron balcony. The large red room was already swarming with art lovers when Angie and Lila arrived, but Bobby spotted them right away and came over to welcome them. He was a handsome man, six foot three, with auburn hair, dressed in a perfectly cut blazer, and an open-necked striped shirt. Aware that he had seen them enter and so as not to look too eager, Lila turned her attention to the wall and was looking carefully at a painting when he came up to them.

"Well, Dr. Jones and Lila Williams! What an honor to have you both here! Lila, I had no idea you were home. Are you and Philip moving back?"

"I may be, but I don't know Philip's plans," Lila blurted out.

"Oh, I'm sorry to hear that. Maybe you and Angie will join me for dinner at Commander's after the show."

"We can't," Angie said. "Another time, but tonight, we have plans."

Bobby said he was sorry and moved on to greet other guests. Lila stared at Angie, swallowing her anger. "And what plans do we have, Doctor?"

"There's only one plan, and that is *not* to rile this city up with gossip the minute you get home."

"God, Angie. Dinner with a group of people after an art opening isn't much to gossip about." The room was comfortably air conditioned, but Lila felt hot. She pushed her hair behind her ears.

"You forget *where* you are and *who* you are, let alone who Bobby is. You've been living in

Tokyo for five years, which makes *you* interesting, and Bobby is the town's richest bachelor, which makes *him* interesting." Angie's right index finger was not pointing at Lila's face, but rather in the direction of her shoes. It was pointing though.

Heaving an exasperated sigh, Lila allowed herself to sulk a few minutes longer.

The two women accepted the offer of white wine from a casually dressed waiter and started to inspect the paintings, which were abstract mixed media in sensational Fauve colors. The paint application gave them an interesting texture that Angie and Lila liked.

Bobby brought the artist, Vivian Bruns, over to meet Lila and Angie, saying that they were his sister's two best friends from school. Lila took note of the artist's skimpy black dress and said, "Angie and I were just saying how much we like your paintings, Vivian. Is this your first one-man show?"

"Oh, God, no, but this gallery has sex appeal. It suits me. It suits my work."

"Well, good luck with the show, and we hope to see you again while you are here," Angie said before they moved on to mingle with the others.

As they continued to feign interest in the paintings, Lila saw many familiar faces and was soothed by the unique sound of New Orleans, honey melting into the vowels, sweetening and softening them. She ate the buttery roasted pecans and laughed at a friend's comment on the artist's evident self-satisfaction. She watched Bobby pay more attention than was strictly necessary to this elongated brunette and hoped her show would be a flop.

After the first hour, a local band arrived, and Angie was persuaded to sing. Her advanced degree in medicine did nothing to diminish her crowd appeal, and Lila had the great pleasure of seeing the artist upstaged.

After the set was over, Lila caught Angie's eye and gave her the let's-get-out-of-here-right-now look and pointed to the door. They decided to go on to Chez Hélène, just a ten-minute drive from Bobby's gallery.

Tuesday nights are fairly slow at Chez Hélène, and the women were seated right away. Though it's not an elegant place, it is very popular as the food is both delicious and reasonably priced. Glancing at the menu, they both ordered fried chicken, collard greens, and potato salad.

Angie put her elbows on the table and leaned in toward her friend. "Now that we have some peace and quiet, tell me more about Philip."

"Angie, I just don't know what happened to the Philip I married. His drinking was getting worse and worse, and that night with Charlie was the last straw."

"Alcoholism is a strange disease, Lila, and Ricky was right in saying that it *is* a disease. It's sort of like diabetes in respect to the body's inability to process sugar. I don't understand the pathology well enough to explain it, but I can tell you one thing, it takes fine people with good intentions and brings them down."

"Of course, Philip would deny that he has a problem," Lila interjected.

"Well, denial is a natural defense mechanism. It was identified by Freud and studied more thoroughly by Jung. But what's weird about it is that like sleep, you don't know you're doing it until you stop doing it. And like sleep, you can slip right back again. I think this is why Alcoholics Anonymous is so effective. They keep reminding the person there's a problem."

"Do you think I could I get Philip to go to A.A.?"

"I don't think you can. I've heard alcoholism has to be self-diagnosed, but this is way out of my field. The pastor of my church knows a lot about addiction though. Or you could go to a shrink."

"What would you do?"

"I'd go to Pastor Jim. He helped me after the accident. I was one angry, hate-filled, black woman. I screamed so much Dr. Carden thought I'd done permanent damage to my vocal cords. They healed though, and I healed. Pastor Jim helped me see things in a different light and forgive the man who killed my family."

"Sounds like an amazing man."

"He is. He told me to imagine the driver as a little boy wanting to grow up to be a hero. He told me to forgive this little boy who never wanted to be a drunk driver. It helped me a lot to see it like this. I don't know if that makes any sense to you."

"Well, it's interesting."

"Pastor Jim says we can't forgive sin. Only God can forgive sin, but we need to forgive the sinner somehow. I forgave the little boy, not the man he had become."

"Did it help you that the driver was killed in the accident too?"

"No. His living or dying wouldn't have changed a thing. What the accident changed was me. I went from a blues singer to a pediatric surgeon. Right now, you have an abusive addict on your hands, and whatever happens, you will be stronger and wiser because of this." Angie fiddled with her ring. It was the diamond one Claude had given her. She wore it on her right hand now.

"I've actually gotten to know that man's widow. He was a high school football coach. She said he was a wonderful man, except a couple of times a year he went on these benders and became a monster."

Looking at her friend with compassion, Angie continued, "I know you're worried about Philip. The man you married is still there somewhere, and maybe he will wake up and maybe he won't.

It takes a lot of courage to change. I have no idea if Philip has that courage, but there is mysterious power in prayer. We can pray for Philip tonight, if you'd like."

"Not here in the restaurant!"

"No, of course not! Later, at your house, or I'll go with you to Trinity Church if you'd be more comfortable there. Or you could go to New Hope Baptist and talk to Jim."

"I'd better warn you, I haven't prayed in a long time, Angie."

"God will be glad to hear from you, Lila, and remember, he doesn't hold grudges."

CHAPTER

3

From the Parker's house on State Street, it is a short drive down St. Charles Avenue to the Convent of the Sacred Heart, which houses the school where the three women met in first grade. Lila drove through the black wrought-iron gates, admiring the massive yet elegant red brick building shaded by ancient magnolias. Driving halfway around the circle, she parked in front of the fountain. Listening to the water play, she lingered on the steps and let nostalgia wash over her, thinking of all the good friends she had made here in her schooldays and of all the women who had made a difference in her life.

Mother Fitzpatrick was sitting at the reception desk on the left as she entered the building. Springing up and embracing Lila, the old nun said, "Oh, Lila, I was delighted when Sister Deborah told me you would be coming to see her today. You look beautiful as always."

"Mother Fitz, I'm so happy to see you too. You haven't changed a bit." Lila squeezed both of the nun's hands in hers.

"Well, there've been a few changes around here, but you'll still know your way around. Wait in the visitor's room, and I'll tell Sister Deborah you're here. I know she's anxious to see you."

Crossing the entrance hall to the cozy sitting room, Lila sat on a low Victorian sofa. Debo arrived a few moments later with a swish of swirling garments and arms held out to Lila. "Hooray! You're here! I want to hear everything and tell everything at once."

Relieved to see that Debo looked quite normal, the drab dress doing nothing to hide her startling beauty or the pulchritude beneath, Lila hugged Debo and laughed nervously. Since

Debo left for MIT and Lila for Columbia, they had gone their separate ways, seeing each other only on vacations and keeping in touch mainly through Angie.

"Is this an interview with the astronomer-nun for the *New York Times*?" Debo's eyebrows shot up.

"No interviews. In fact, I am officially on leave of absence. So don't worry about being quoted."

"Good because I don't want any of this getting back to the Pope." Debo furrowed her brow in horror.

"Oh, Debo. Tell me about your life. What was the turning point?"

"You don't sound like you are on leave to me, Lila, but I know you are curious to know why I'm becoming a nun. Two reasons. One: empiric evidence that I pick the wrong men. Two: E does, in fact, equal mc squared."

"I beg your pardon." Lila was taken aback. Was this a reason for becoming a nun?

"Well, you know, I have always made the worst decisions about men, starting when they were still very young boys."

"Yes, I do remember some terrible choices. But what does Einstein have to do with it?"

"Well, let me explain. You know that what we see isn't real. It's just whirling molecules. Time doesn't exist in any real sense, and when you look at the stars, some of them have been dead for millions of years, yet we still see the light." Lila could see that Debo was warming up to her subject.

Shifting in her chair, Debo turned to face Lila directly. "Science cannot prove or disprove God, and for some reason, people today are only interested in the Big Bang and not the Big Banger. Emphasis is on how the universe evolved, not why. This stopped making sense to me."

"Well, go on, Debo, don't leave me hanging."

"You see, I got on very well without God during my undergraduate years at MIT, only going to church when my parents were visiting or when I was home. Then, I started working on my master's degree, and there were several Buddhists in my section. They became good friends, and I became interested in Buddhism and started practicing Zen meditation." Debo pressed her palms together and bowed her head slightly.

Smiling as Lila returned the gesture, Debo continued, "I studied and practiced on a regular basis for months before I realized I could be a good Buddhist and a good Christian at the same time. All of that was well and good, but I started getting these uncomfortable feelings that I was meant to dedicate my life to God. I didn't like these feelings one bit and started medicating them with Jack Daniels. One morning, I woke up in bed with my spherical trigonometry professor, and I thought to myself, *That's it. I am giving up Jack and taking up God.*"

"Just like that?" Lila asked.

"Not quite. There were some unusual occurrences, which got my attention, and I started going back to church on the sly. Being a practicing Catholic at MIT would have been way too radically countercultural in 2005, even for me." Debo waved her hand dismissively.

"I got my master's in astrophysics and went to work at NASA, but without the Jack Daniels, the 'call' got louder. I tried to ignore it, unsuccessfully, as you can see." Debo raised her shoulders, turned her palms up helplessly, and smiled.

"Would you call what you referred to as 'unusual occurrences' supernatural experiences?"

"Since I believe in God, I think of these experiences as being natural ones, but they'd be very hard to explain. It's not that I don't want to talk about these things, but I just don't want to talk about them now. I have a class in fifteen minutes, and I want to hear about you." Debo settled back into her chair.

Lila stiffened and began, "Well, the twins were born six months after we arrived in Japan, and I had a wonderful older Japanese woman to look after them, which allowed me to continue writing and have some free time."

Debo looked interested, and Lila continued, "It was difficult at first, but I became intrigued by the Japanese culture. I went to every lecture in English at the Tokyo National Museum. I studied ikebana and even made a few Japanese friends, though my command of the language is still shaky. We traveled quite a bit, but always in Asia. The international community in Tokyo is full of interesting people—"

"Lila, do you want to tell me what's really on your mind, or do you want me to guess?"

"Oh, Debo, it's Philip. It was too dangerous for us to stay there with him. He's drinking too much and using cocaine. That's why I brought the twins home. We're staying at Mother and Daddy's."

"I'm so sorry, Lila. I had no idea, but addiction does seem to be the plague of our time. Listen, I would love to talk to you more about this. You know, there are solutions. Are you free on Saturday? Right now, I have to go. My students will be waiting for me."

"Can you come and meet the twins? We could all have lunch with Angie."

"I'd love that. Can you pick me up around noon?"

"Angie or I will be here at noon on Saturday."

When they hugged each other, there was no more nervous laughter, and Lila left her friend, feeling that the old intimacy had been restored. It astonished her how that bond, forged early in life, could be reestablished so quickly.

CHAPTER

4

That Thursday morning, Angie drove over to the Parker's house to pick up Lila and the twins. Angie parked in front of the garage and went around to ring the front doorbell. Standing, waiting at the door, she noticed that the stucco was cracking in places and the house could use a coat of fresh paint. She had always felt welcome in this house and hoped that the Parkers were not falling on hard times. Mr. Parker answered the door and gave Angie a warm hug and said that Mrs. Parker was sorry not to be home, but it was her day to work with Debo's mother at the animal shelter.

The twins were blond and blue-eyed, like Lila, but with Philip's sharply defined features. Both were shy with restless eyes. Charlie's black eye had lightened to green and yellow. Angie gave it a quick professional look. "Seems like you had quite a shiner there, Charlie."

"Yeah. It was black and purple before. I got in Dad's way."

"Well, you are not in *my* way. How 'bout coming with me to the zoo and having a picnic in the park?"

Angie and Lila struggled to put the car seats into Angie's car so the twins could ride in the back of her convertible. The top was down, and the twins were thrilled. Once they'd backed out of the driveway, Charlie and Charlotte lost their shyness and began singing in Japanese.

The small zoo had a petting area for little children. The twins were excited and, taking Angie's hands, made a beeline for the bunnies. All four of them were happy to be right where they were. Angie did not have to be at St. Joseph's until three o'clock, so they had plenty of time for their picnic under the Spanish moss-laden oaks. Lila was struck that so many of these magnificent old trees had survived Hurricane Katrina. They found a spot and dove into the picnic hamper Angie's Aunt May had packed. Peanut butter and jelly sandwiches on white bread for the twins. This was a first for them. Angie was dumbfounded they had never had peanut butter and jelly sandwiches before, and Lila at how much they loved them.

"Lila, how did you find Debo after all these years?" Angie was munching on a chicken salad sandwich.

"She's as funny and beautiful as ever. I suggested that we have lunch with her and the twins on Saturday. Is that good for you?"

"Saturday's perfect for me."

"Where should we go?"

"Debo will want to go to Manale's for the oysters, but I don't know how Charlie and Charlotte will like that."

"They'll love it. Don't forget they were brought up on sushi and sashimi. Raw oysters will be ho-hum for them, but it's August. You can't eat oysters in August."

"It'll be September by Saturday. Labor Day weekend, remember?"

"Oh, right." Lila was thinking about their trip to Paris after senior year. "Will you ever forget our trip to Paris? How Debo's parents managed to rent a car for three eighteen-year-olds, I'll never know."

"And once Debo got behind that wheel, passengers and pedestrians were in for it! Debo, smoking two cigarettes at once, screeching at all the Parisians in her flawed French."

Through her laughter, Angie continued, "How many times did we circle the Arc de Triomphe trying to get out of there? And the looks on the faces of the other drivers when they got a load of double-cigarette Debo bearing down on them! God, I'd love to go there again."

"And all the boys. Debo was certainly a magnet for them, and Frenchmen are so gallant. So much more appreciative of women than our guys are. And remember Debo saying, 'Girls! Elbows in, tits up!'

"Crazy. Let's go back next year to celebrate our thirtieth birthdays."

"Wouldn't it be strange with Debo a nun?" Lila leaned over to wipe Charlie's face with a white paper napkin.

"Not strange, just different. Debo makes things happen. There's never a dull moment with her. I envy her students. You just know those girls' minds are being blown every day.

"By the way, I hope you don't mind, I made an appointment with Pastor Jim for you this afternoon at four and, just because it is a black church doesn't mean you're not welcome."

"Doesn't it seem weird for me to talk to him? Not knowing him, I mean, or even being a Baptist?"

"Most things are weirder, Lila. Anyway, you can choose—a minister or a shrink. Take your pick, but you need to talk to someone who has some kind of experience with addicts. Have you heard from Philip yet?"

"I had a garbled message on my cell. Something about 'love' and 'twins' and 'bitch.'"

"Well, why don't you talk to Pastor Jim before you call him back? I know he can help you. I've gotten to know him well over the past five years.

I sing in his choir, and of course, he was there at the time of the accident. He's a wise man."

———◦———

Mrs. Parker had returned home early from the animal shelter and was waiting for Lila and the twins. She offered to stay with the twins so Lila could go to meet Angie's pastor.

Driving well below the speed limit, Lila headed out for the appointment. She was not looking forward to talking to a perfect stranger about her marriage, even one Angie knew and trusted. She had thought about cancelling but decided to drive on, thinking at this point it would be rude to Angie not to go.

"Lila Williams! You're so welcome here," came the booming voice before she had even closed the car door. "Come this way." Pastor Jim was a big man of about fifty, clean-shaven, and neatly dressed. "Angie's a special friend of mine, and you're her lifelong friend. So we're connected already." He walked Lila through a covered passageway on the right side of the church into his small office. "Have a seat." He waved her to an armchair across from his battered oak desk.

There were orderly stacks of papers covering all the flat surfaces and overfilled bookshelves behind him. His chair creaked as he sat down.

"Pastor Jim, Angie told me how helpful and kind you were at the time of the accident. I still feel bad that I wasn't here for her. I had just had twins and was living in Tokyo." Lila crossed her arms in front of her chest and shrank into the chair.

"Yes, she told me you write articles for the *New York Times*. She also told me your marriage is a little threadbare."

Well, here's a man who gets straight to the point, Lila thought.

"I don't know where to start."

"No one ever does, Lila. Why don't you tell me why you married Philip, what you loved about him?" Pastor Jim pulled his chair closer to the desk and leaned on his forearms, looking Lila right in the eye.

Lila spent the next half hour recounting all the things she loved about Philip. She talked about their courtship in New York when she was a student at Columbia, and he a young lawyer at Asher, Clarke, in Manhattan. She talked about their shared interest in the theatre and how they had acted in amateur productions. She laughed remembering how Philip had fumbled his lines after too little sleep and how he often skipped rehearsals due to work. She said he was romantic and that he sometimes arrived at her door holding one of those silly balloons that says "I love you." She told him that Philips's endless knowledge of the world had made her feel secure. And then, she started talking about the effect alcohol and drugs had on their lives. It was hopeless trying not to cry, but she carried on with her narrative. Pastor Jim never took his eyes off her and never interrupted.

"I just want him back like he was," Lila wailed, accepting the Kleenex he offered.

"There's no going back, Lila, but you may find you have a better man at the end of all of this, if Philip is brave enough to break free from the prison of addiction."

"But for him, it's more of a playground than a prison. It's his form of freedom."

"Let me assure you, addiction is *not* freedom."

"Who's going to tell him that?"

"I don't know, but God knows. Before you leave, let's pray for Philip."

Lila bowed her head, squirming a little. For some reason, she felt embarrassed.

"Almighty God, look with mercy on your son Philip. Open his eyes to see himself. Bless him with courage. And give Lila the comfort of knowing she's not alone, that you have promised to be with her during her troubles. Guide and protect this family. I pray this in the mighty name of Jesus. Amen."

"Amen. Thank you, Pastor." Relieved to have this over with, Lila got up to leave. She realized she had done most of the talking, but his few words had been profound.

Pastor Jim walked her to the car, and as she was opening the door, he said to her, "Let me know if you want me to talk to Philip."

"Philip's in Tokyo, Pastor."

"Well, don't be surprised if he turns up here. It seems to me you people have a deep connection. The Almighty works in mysterious ways, his wonders to perform. Something will happen, Lila." Pastor Jim's confidence was contagious, almost convincing Lila that something unexpected might indeed happen.

"I bet a good convent girl like you knows how to pray. So pray for Philip, and I will too."

"Thank you again, Pastor. You have given me some hope. I'll tell you what, when I came here, I had no hope left after all these years of trying."

As Lila was starting the car, she thought about what Pastor Jim had just said and realized she was not ready to trust any of her decisions to God. God had been absent from her thoughts for a good ten years now, and she had been just fine without him.

As she drove off, she tuned into WNOE and started singing along with the oldies. And then, Elvis's voice filled the car singing "Amazing Grace." Her throat felt tight and her eyes prickled, but she sang along through her sobs, knowing that somehow now she was committed to doing her part if Philip wanted to recover. But that was a big *if.*

CHAPTER

5

The storm started late Friday night. By noon on Saturday, the winds were over fifty miles an hour and raindrops the size of marbles were smashing into the streets, bouncing back up to join others pouring down. Since the twins were content with their cartoons, Lila decided to leave them with her parents instead of taking them to the restaurant in this weather. There was no hurry since Angie was picking up Debo. Lila pulled on her mother's yellow rain gear and slipped her cell, lipstick, and credit card in the pocket. Borrowing her father's black Lexus, she headed for Napoleon Avenue.

Driving down the wide expanse of St. Charles Avenue, windshield wipers beating furiously, Lila was blinded by a fork of lightning shooting down the streetcar tracks. She heard a thud. Stamping on the brakes, she lurched forward and skidded onto the sidewalk. "Oh, God, no!" she was screaming as she flung open the car door and fought her way through the thick sheets of rain. There, to her left, was a body. A woman's body. And she was not moving.

Lila felt for a pulse. In her panic, she was unable to feel anything. *Please don't be dead!* Still crouching next to the body, she called 911. Car lights were coming down the avenue. She redialed 911 to ask whether she should move the body out of the street but heard the sirens before she had finished the question. The police car turned expertly, blocking the traffic, lights flashing, siren shrieking.

Lila was bundled into the back of the squad car. Moaning quietly, she rocked backward and forward, alone in the car with only the deafening drumming of the rain on the roof to comfort her.

In the distance, she heard an ambulance scream-ing its way from Touro Hospital. Several eons seemed to pass before she could make out the lights. *Oh, God, no. I've killed her.* Twitching with fear, she remembered Charlie's black eye and imagined the twins looking at her blankly, not recognizing her at the end of her prison time.

The door opened a crack and someone said, "Ma'am, just to let you know, the victim has regained consciousness. We'll know more in a few minutes." The sound of the stranger's voice roused her enough to think of calling Angie at the restaurant. Angie answered on the first ring. Lila croaked, "I've run over a woman. Come to the riverside of St. Charles and Octavia right away. Bring Debo."

By the time Angie and Debo arrived fifteen minutes later, the ambulance was just pull-ing out. The cops were questioning Lila in the squad car, her father's dented car now stranded near the front steps of a raised cottage with dark red shutters.

Angie banged on the passenger window of the squad car. "Officer, I'm a doctor and a friend of Mrs. Williams'." The cops looked at each other.

The officer in the passenger seat rolled down the window an inch and said, "This isn't protocol, but get in the back, Doctor."

Sliding in next to her trembling friend, Angie put a protective arm around Lila's shoulders. "Don't you worry, honey, everything will be fine."

The officer in the passenger seat turned, "I'm Lieutenant Sanders, and my partner here is Sergeant Lane. I'm sorry, but there are certain formalities, which need to be taken care of at the station, and Mrs. Williams must come with us. You're welcome to come with her. Is there someone else in your car, ma'am?"

"Yes, Lieutenant. Sister Deborah of the Sacred Heart Convent." Angie straightened her back as if perfect posture or at least better posture just might improve the situation.

"Then, if Sister Deborah can drive a car, she can follow us."

"Oh, she can drive a car all right, Lieutenant. I'm just not sure I want her driving *my* car—in all this rain. Could she ride with you? I'll drive my car and meet you at the station. Is it the one on Magazine Street?"

"Yes. Second District."

Angie and Debo changed cars. Hitting the cool dry interior of the squad car, a haze of steam rose from Debo's clothes. With one arm firmly around Lila's shoulder, Debo turned to the lieutenant and said, "Oh my goodness, Sam Sanders. I'm Debo Reeve."

"Debo, my God. What happened to you?"

"Well, you might say God happened. And what's a big shot like you doing cruising around in a storm like this?"

"Just looking for you, Debo."

***

Sitting in the large front room of the police station, Lila, Angie, and Debo waited for Lila's turn to make her statement. The desk sergeant sat behind a counter facing the door, phones and pads of forms close at hand. Lieutenant Sanders made sure Lila had a blanket and provided towels and coffee for all three before going back out on patrol. Lila's teeth were still chattering, partly due to the shock and partly due to the powerful air conditioning. Angie had a towel turban on her head and one draped around her shoulders.

She turned to Debo and asked, "How do you know the lieutenant?"

"Oh, I dated the DA for a few minutes a couple of years ago. Sam's a friend of his."

Angie shook her head, smiling. She still couldn't quite reconcile the Debo she used to know with this woman sitting next to her, now almost a nun.

"And you," Debo said, turning a question back to her, "do you still know anyone at Touro?"

"Yeah, most of the staff from my residency days are still there. Why don't I call ER and see what I can get out of them?" She headed off to the ladies' room to find some privacy.

Lila called her father at home and told him she was fine and then handed the phone to Debo who explained what had happened and assured him that there was nothing to worry about and no reason to come to the Station. Lila paced in circles, water squirting out of her shoes, chilling her naked feet.

The station was surprisingly busy for lunchtime on Saturday. The sound of voices, phones ringing, and the static accompanying the dispatcher's voice on the walkie-talkies could be heard in the background. At one point, a scantily dressed woman came in shaking the rain off her umbrella and went directly to the desk sergeant who said, "Hey, Shanna, what can we do for you today?"

"Hey, Sergeant. It's 'bout Leeroy."

"It's always about Leeroy, Shanna."

"This time it's worse."

"It always gets worse."

"I demand police protection."

"The NOPD can't get involved with your private affairs, Shanna."

"Well, as long as you know it's your fault when I turn up dead."

"You don't have to go back, Shanna. You have the address if you really want protection."

"Shuh, I won't go there. You guys got to protect me in my own home."

"That lease is in Leeroy's name, and you know it."

"Don't nobody do the job 'round this place."

"You have the address, Shanna. You choose."

"How you guys stand it? It's freezing in here."

"Help yourself to coffee, and I'll see you tomorrow."

"If I live through this day."

"See you, Shanna."

Lila was still in shock and didn't seem to notice all of this coming and going. But when Angie came back with the news from Touro, she seemed to snap back. "It's okay," Angie whispered. "Only a broken ankle. But she's in hysterics. Don't let on to anyone here that I called."

Silently waiting, they watched a tall man in an old-fashioned black suit march in the front door. Though his goatee was dripping, he had the look of someone who had just strolled over from a mansion in the Garden District.

"Sergeant," he said, walking stiffly up to the counter, "the lights are out at the White House."

The sergeant glanced up from his paperwork. "But, Mr. President, there's a generator at the White House. Let me call and make sure everything's okay." He pushed a button and speed dialed a number. "Hello, this is Sergeant Manice. The president of the United States is here at the Station. He says the lights are out at the White

House." He listened to someone at the other end and said, "Very good," and hung up.

"Mr. President, they say you're needed back at the White House. The vice president is on his way to pick you up. In fact, look behind you. Here he is now."

A huge black man came in carrying a golf umbrella. He nodded to the sergeant and calmly took the tall man by the elbow to usher him out.

The three women looked at each other and giggled. For just a moment, Lila forgot the trauma of the last hour.

Lieutenant Sanders arrived with dough-nuts and apologies that they were still waiting. Because of the weather, there was a backlog of traffic incidents. He assured them that it would not be more than another half hour's wait. Angie noticed how good he looked in his uniform and wished there was a hair dryer at the police station so she could restore herself.

"Sam, you just missed the president." Debo laughed.

"Oh, that would be President Lincoln. He escapes from his keepers and comes here to check on us. His family owns some kind of candy company, and they send us ten-pound boxes of chocolates from time to time to sweeten us up. He's harmless enough."

"Well, we're in no hurry," Debo said. "It's quite an education sitting here. Actually, I'm worried about a young lady named Shanna."

"Don't worry about her, Debo. She's in no real danger. She just likes our coffee."

Just then, Lila's name was called, and the three women were escorted into a small room in the back. Lila made a statement and gave her contact information. The officer said Prytania Wrecking and Towing had Mr. Parker's car and would call him when it was ready to be picked up.

As they were leaving, Lieutenant Sanders stepped out of his office to say good-bye. "Oh, Sam, please stay in touch. I'm usually available at the convent between three and five."

"Let's hope there won't be any charges pressed against Mrs. Williams. I'll call as soon as I have more information. It's great to see you again, Debo. See you soon, I hope."

"And if there is anything I can do, Lieutenant, you can reach me at St. Joseph's," added Angie. Debo noticed Sam's face light up.

"Ladies, ya'll take real good care of yourselves. And drive safely."

CHAPTER

6

L ate that afternoon, Lila got the call from Sam Sanders saying there would be no charges pressed. Angie had already called her with the information she had managed to wheedle out of her friends in ER. Apparently, Maria Sanchez, a forty-seven-year-old native of Mexico City, arrived in New Orleans in February and was living with some cousins while looking for a job in the hotel industry. No one was hiring. She was now living off the generosity of the Jehovah's Witnesses. This wasn't the first time Angie had heard of the Witnesses helping their people.

Maria told the medic who was translating for her that all she wanted now was to go back home to Mexico and that she would never jaywalk again.

When Lila called Debo to pass on this information, Debo suggested her mother might want to help. "My mother has way too much time and money on her hands. And she's good at this kind of thing."

"I think my parents could help too."

"Don't be selfish, Lila. My mother *needs* Maria."

"Well, let's wait and see what happens."

Early on Sunday morning, while the twins were downstairs watching cartoons, Lila sat at the desk in her childhood room. The room had not changed since her freshman year in college. The white wallpaper with apple green bows and matching curtains were still there along with the white matchstick shades. A few of her old stuffed animals lounged on the queen-sized bed. It was dated, but she loved it. She felt safe here.

She just got a message on her cell from Tokyo. It must have come in during the night. Philip's boss himself had called. Alarm signals were pulsing through her already shot nervous system. Why would Robert Hardy be calling her?

She sat at that white wicker desk, twirling her hair around her finger, staring at the phone. Fourteen hours time difference meant it would now be 10:00 p.m. in Tokyo. This was obviously an emergency. Otherwise, why would he call? Could Philip have run over someone too? After a few moments' hesitation, Lila succumbed to the inevitable and dialed the number.

"Robert Hardy," answered the smooth, patrician voice.

"Mr. Hardy, I'm sorry to call so late. This is Lila Williams calling from New Orleans. I just got your message." Lila was barely breathing, fearing the worst.

"Lila, do you have a moment? This is a difficult subject to discuss on the phone."

"Go ahead, sir."

"As you've probably noticed, Philip hasn't been himself for several months. We would've talked to you first about sending him to the Anderson Center, which is an alcohol and drug rehabilitation facility near Los Angeles. But since you're out of the country and we wanted to act quickly, we talked to Philip directly. He left this afternoon on an American Airlines flight. An associ- ate from our office is escorting him."

"I'm sure you made the right decision, Mr. Hardy." Lila could feel her shoulders and spine unclench. She willed herself to match his cool, detached tone, though she was shocked that he and probably everyone in the firm now knew about Philip's problem.

"I have spoken with some people at Anderson, and as part of the program, you, as his wife and next of kin, will be asked to go there in three weeks to stay for five days. Is that okay with you? Do you have someone who can look after your children?"

"Yes, sir. That won't be a problem." Lila's heart was racing. Until now, she had only met Hardy on formal occasions wearing her severely cut black Armani suit. She admired this hand- some older man. He had the reputation of being the best American lawyer in Asia. He spoke Japanese like a native, having spent seven years of his childhood in Japan while his father was U.S. ambassador. Though he was based in New York, Lila had heard about his spectacular resi- dence in Tokyo, although she had never been invited. Now suddenly, this man was involved in her personal life.

"I trust this will help Philip. I like Philip personally, and Asher, Clarke wants him back as we remember him. He's a valuable asset to the firm."

"Yes, Philip is very lucky to be given this chance. Thank you, Mr. Hardy."

Hardy gave Lila the phone number of the Anderson Center and the names of two contact people there. She put down the phone and breathed deeply. *So this is it*, she thought to herself. This is the turning point. Now everyone knows. Before she had time to change her mind, she picked up the phone and called L.A. Yes, she would come to Family Week. Yes, she would be available by phone at any time. Yes, she understood that Philip and she could not have any contact until then.

Hanging up the phone, Lila was reluctant to put her pen down as if by hanging on to it she could turn back time. She sat with her elbows on the desk, imagining just exactly how awkward this whole reunion would be.

Later that afternoon, the phone rang. It was Angie. "Whoa, I had a great time last night!

That fine lieutenant took me to Chez Hélène for dinner."

"Get out! Tell me all about it."

"Well, he's from Clinton, and Aunt May knows his family for one thing, and we share an interest in gospel music for another. He sang in the choir at Asbury Methodist Church when he was a kid. That was my father's family church."

"Sounds good. What else?"

"He's thirty-five and never been married, thank God, and has been with the NOPD for twelve years. He came to New Hope this morning and took me out to lunch, and tonight, we're going out for a fancy dinner. Is that enough news for one day?"

"Angie! That's great!"

"It is great. I can't believe how well we got on. There were none of those awkward silences, and he can really make me laugh." Angie's happiness made Lila smile. "Anything new with you, girl?"

"Philip's boss called. They're on to him. He's on his way to a rehab in L.A."

"Oh my God. Tell me what happened."

"I don't really know. All I know is that he agreed to go and is on his way out there right now. He must have lost it at the office. I can't imagine him going to work trashed, but something dramatic must've happened for them to send him off like this."

"What does this mean for you, honey?" Angie could tell that Lila had not processed this information and was still in shock from yesterday's accident. Her heart softened for her friend who was clearly in deep distress.

"I have to go there for Family Week, whatever that is, at the end of the month. In the meantime, I'm not supposed to contact him, not that I want to."

"You'll be able to do whatever it is you have to do when the time comes, Lila."

"Thanks, Ange, for always being so supportive. Now, you go doodle yourself up for tonight, and don't worry about me." *But who is going to worry about me?* Lila wondered.

CHAPTER

7

Ned Kirby sat in the business class seat next to Philip on the afternoon American Airlines flight from Tokyo to L.A. The attendant had just brought Philip his third martini and was clearing the dessert. "Is there anything else I can get you, sir?"

"How about another one of these?" Philip pointed to his drink.

The two lawyers had been colleagues for the past five years, but the truth was Ned had never liked Philip and resented that Philip had been made partner, while he was still an associate. He was jealous of Philip's popularity with everyone from the mailroom to the boardroom, jealous of his easy rapport with Asians and Americans alike, and it irked him to sit silent next to Philip for the twelve-hour flight. Ned would far rather have been back in Tokyo. But he knew he could somehow make this trip work to his advantage.

Burying himself in his computer, Ned watched Philip from the corner of his eye. Philip had a haunted look on his finely chiseled face; his short light-brown hair was mussed. His hazel eyes were bloodshot; he looked too tall and too thin for the seat, gangly like a young colt. Placed on the table next to his martini, Philip's own computer stayed closed.

Looking forward to unloading Philip at Anderson and spending a few days of vacation time in L.A., Ned wondered why Asher, Clarke thought Philip Williams was worth all this expense. He was just as good a lawyer as Philip, and what he lacked in the way of a Harvard law degree, he made up for in shrewdness. While cleaning up after Philip's increasingly sloppy work, he had watched him deteriorate, eyeing his own chance for promotion.

Three days ago, when Philip showed up wasted at work, Ned had personally made sure that Philip blundered into Robert Hardy's office. Now, he had entire month to plot Philip's downfall. Pretty soon, he would take his place. Ned smiled as he thought how easy it would be to take this soft-spoken Southern boy down. Almost too easy. He remembered switching some grades junior year in high school. For him, it made all the difference. None of nuns ever suspected, and once he got going, lying and cheating became second nature to him.

After stumbling through customs at LAX with Ned guiding him to the waiting limousine, Philip looked out of the window, a concentrated look on his face. "L.A.'s an architectural nervous breakdown. Look at this mess. What *were* they thinking?" Ned didn't reply. It looked good to him. Fan and date palms swayed gracefully over emerald lawns. Philip commented on palms being water hogs, but otherwise, the two men were silent during the ten-mile journey to the exclusive northern suburb where the Anderson Center was located.

As they pulled up to the gate, it slid open to allow the limousine to enter the walled compound. The main building was white stucco with a red Spanish tile roof. The other buildings were various sizes with the same architectural style, connected by flagstone paths winding through carefully maintained grounds.

The driver pulled Philip's suitcase out of the trunk and walked around to open the door. Ned, relieved to see the back of his colleague, managed a polite good-bye, though he wasn't sure if Philip heard.

Though still slurring his words during his intake interview, Philip tried hard to sober up. Wanting to come across as a sensible, cooperative man, he asked for coffee and explained he was unable to sleep on the plane. The intake office was clean and practical, and the interviewer asked questions in a detached, nonjudgmental way. Philip openly admitted that he had drunk on average a quart of gin a day and had used cocaine several times a week over the past six months. Acknowledging that all this had been building up for about ten years, he didn't bother to lie and signed all the papers as quickly as possible, just so he could move on to his room and get some sleep.

After the interview was finally over, Philip was taken to the detox unit. The nurses were busy with other clients, but when Philip came in, they found time to search his bag, removing his mouthwash, Blackberry, and computer. Mouthwash was not allowed as it contains alcohol. His Blackberry and computer would be safely locked up and returned after his stay in primary care. Panicked by the loss of his Blackberry, Philip thought of asking how long this would be, but in the end, he didn't have enough energy. More papers had to be signed and receipts given. His eyes were like lead. Without cocaine to stimulate him, the martinis on the plane had knocked him out. Samples of his bodily fluids had to be taken. *Christ, won't these people ever stop?* Philip's sleep-deprived body screamed for mercy.

By the time he got to his room, he was too exhausted to shower. He tossed his clothes on the floor and collapsed onto the narrow bed. Before he passed out, he thought about Charlie and Charlotte. Would he ever see them again?

He didn't know if he hated Lila or himself more. He heard the nurse asking if he needed something to help him sleep. "No, but thank you," he mumbled.

At the hotel on Rodeo Drive, Ned thought about his plan. He had always wanted to distance himself from his Brooklyn background and speak in that "from nowhere in particular" way that national newscasters speak. Being here now in Los Angeles was just the time and place for this.

He got the name of a speech coach from the limousine driver who, like so many service industry employees in L.A., happened to be an out-of-work actor. Ned looked the name up on his Blackberry and called to make an appointment for the next morning.

When it came down to it, Ned was not an unsophisticated guy. He had gone to Fordham and NYU Law School on scholarships and had graduated near the top of his class a few years back. Being part of the Asher, Clarke team in Asia was a big step up and going to Tokyo suited him just fine. He wanted out of New York where he had few friends and little contact with his family. Over the years, he had somehow managed to alienate his siblings and fall out with his mother. He never told her he was leaving for Tokyo, but at the last moment, he decided to drop by. She was standing outside the apartment building chatting to the super. Shocked, all she could do was wish him luck and say a quick good-bye before he hurried off. They had let the years put distance between them.

Like everyone in his family, Ned was smart and good-looking. But he was the first one with a college degree. After that, he hadn't had much time for them, and later on, he even ditched Brenda, sweet, sexy Brenda, who had loved him since junior high. It was thanks to Brenda's salary as a dental hygienist that they were able to live in a Manhattan apartment, dump that it was. During that last year in law school, he began noticing she would not fit in with the kind of life he was learning to want. Once he had the offer from Asher, Clarke, she was no longer useful to him. The breakup was quick and cruel.

Switching on the TV and heaving himself on the king-sized bed, Ned gave a sigh of contentment. The Beverly Wilshire was just the kind of hotel he liked. Luxurious and understated. This is what he wanted his life to be and getting there fast was his only goal, and he was willing and able to do whatever it took.

Phillip's addictions, their boss's sense of fairness, the sixteen-hour time change between Tokyo and L.A. were all working in his favor. Ned got up and fastidiously unpacked his cheap suitcase. It won't be long now. Just a matter of time.

Philip woke up in the detox unit, hands shaking and an all too familiar headache. He swung his legs off the bed, staggered to the shower, dressed, and went looking for some Advil at the nurses' station. It was only 5:00 a.m., and everything was still quiet. Philip asked for five Advil, his usual morning dose, but the nurse only gave him two, saying the doctor would be in at ten and assess his case then. "Look, I've got to have my Blackberry to check in with my office."

"Sorry, Philip, it's locked up for now." The nurse looked as if she had said this same thing thousands of times before.

"But you don't understand. I have an important job to do."

"Yes, you do. But it's an inside job, and you won't be needing your Blackberry to do it."

At ten, after trying unsuccessfully to sleep off his headache, Philip was given a small white tablet to settle his nerves. It helped take the edge off but made him feel like he was walking through quicksand. Philip was vaguely aware that these places suggested a stay of at least twenty-eight days. He wondered if yesterday counted as one. He definitely could not be out of touch with the office for such a long time. He had to get his Blackberry back. Also, he thought it was unreasonably extreme to forbid all alcohol. Wine at dinner would be a good way to normalize drinking. After all, people have to live in the real world. He wished he had read the papers he signed yesterday more carefully. He could easily handle his drinking without all this fuss. The mistake was going into Hardy's office the other day, but doesn't everyone make a mistake now and then? How did that happen anyway? And how did being a little bit high get exaggerated into *this*? He wondered what Lila knew. He wanted to rewind the tape by two weeks and play it safe. *What am I doing here?* He wanted a drink.

After four days in detox, just before dinner, Philip was moved into the men's unit, which would become his home for the next four and a half weeks. His room was scrupulously clean with white walls and a cork floor. His roommate, Craig Stein, sat on the bed and watched Philip unload his few belongings into the chest near the window. Craig was twenty-two and had been at Anderson for three weeks. His mother and father had been expected to arrive on Sunday for Family Week. But only his mother had come.

"Yeah, you know. My dad's too busy with his fund. Always busy with that. Anyhow, man, what're you in for?"

"Gin and coke. How about you?"

"Basically, just coke."

"When do I get my computer back?"

"Not yet. They want us to concentrate on what we're here for."

"But I have to be in touch with my office. I have a big deal about to close."

"You remind me of my dad."

Craig took Philip to the dining room at six sharp. He liked to beat the line. The two men crossed the campus, the path flanked by carefully tailored citrus trees. For the first time in a long time, Philip registered a delicate waft of blossoms in the air. He had been asleep most of the time since his arrival and was just beginning to notice his surroundings and to get a look at his fellow inmates. Given the number of tables and chairs, he estimated there would be around eighty or so people expected for dinner. Most of those in line with him were around his age or younger. Surprisingly, none of them looked insane or dangerous. Someone had obviously made an effort to make the place look welcoming. The walls were painted a clear shade of tangerine and were covered in abstract prints in bright primary colors. *A bit like elementary school*, Philip thought.

"What happens after dinner?" Philip asked Craig as they sat down with their trays.

"Depends. If you're scheduled for a 12-Step meeting, you go off campus. Otherwise, you stay here and go to the auditorium. There's always a speaker at seven. At nine, we have a meeting in the unit."

"What kind of meeting?"

"We, like, rehash the day. You know. You can gripe or whatever."

The speaker that evening described how trashed he was before coming to Anderson and how happy he was now after ten years of sobriety. *I am just going to go along with this*, Philip thought to himself. Then a part of him, some voice he didn't recognize began to stir. *Perhaps there is a way out*, it murmured, although only faintly, halfheartedly, like the possibility was only playing a game with him. But then, it is all so tedious, so cant, all these declarations and catchwords. For a moment, he thought of his twins in Louisiana, their sweet-smelling hair, the way they flew at him after work, so full of trust. And he thought of the bottle. The way it waited for him, holding all the answers, the courage, the laughter. Why couldn't he have both?

CHAPTER

8

On Labor Day, Debo went to her parents' house for lunch. Theirs was one of the nicest houses in the Garden District. Built in the 1870s, it was white with dark green shutters and stately Ionic columns. Cut crystal inserts in the front door made rainbow patterns in the sunlight.

Letting herself in with a key, Debo stepped into the spacious entrance hall. She stopped to listen to the activity in the kitchen, appreciating the cool, scented air. Portraits of several generations of Reeves hung on the pale blue walls and marched up the curving staircase, looking down at Debo with indifferent faces. She could hear conversation coming from the paneled library and made her way there, hesitating at the door, not recognizing the female voice.

Bobby was there with Vivian Bruns, the artist who was showing her work at his gallery. Judge and Mrs. Reeve were not yet back from their house in Biloxi, but the Bloody Mary drinking was well underway.

Bobby stood and kissed his sister affectionately on the cheek and introduced her to Vivian.

"So you're the astronomer-nun everyone in this city seems to know!" Vivian was obviously enjoying the Reeve's famous Bloody Marys. The one in her hand was apparently not her first.

"I have a degree in astrophysics, if that's what you mean. But I'm still just a novice at the convent, not yet a fully-fledged nun. And how do you like New Orleans, Vivian? I hear you have a show on."

"Well, it's not New York, but the natives are friendly, and there's plenty to drink." Vivian laughed, signaling to Bobby that she needed a refill.

"Yes. That's one of our claims to fame." Debo caught Bobby's eye. Bobby mimed innocence behind Vivian's back. It was going to be a long lunch.

Debo regretted that Bobby had brought his guest along. She was planning on talking to her mother about Maria Sanchez, sure that she would think of a way to help.

The senior Reeves arrived, proceeded by two barking tan and white King Charles spaniels, Samson and Delilah. Toenails clicking across the marble floor, they raced for the library, bounding straight for Bobby and Debo, waving their feathery tails.

The Reeves were an attractive couple in their early sixties. Mrs. Reeve was in good shape for her age, or so her friends told her. She made sure her hair was restored to its natural auburn color by her hairdresser every three weeks and was disciplined about manicures. She wore a long-sleeved blouse over crisp white pants, silver flats, and large, but simple pearl earrings. As she stepped into the library, she gave off the air of a woman very much in control of her life. One of those rare creatures who seemed to have it all.

Judge Reeve seemed more hesitant though. He was a tall, powerfully built man with a full head of silver hair, wearing a blazer over his golf shirt and carrying a bucket full of yellow roses freshly cut from their garden across the lake. They both had piercing green eyes, which they had passed on to Bobby and Debo.

Someone relieved the judge of the roses. Introductions were made, and they all settled in for a drink before lunch.

"Millicent and I are looking forward to seeing your show, Vivian. We were sorry to miss the opening, but we've been in Biloxi. How long will you be staying in New Orleans?" Ever the perfect gentleman, Judge Reeve hid his disappointment, bending over to pat Samson. In actual fact, he was none too thrilled at having to entertain a stranger from out of town when all he really wanted was a quiet lunch with his children whom he got to see so rarely these days.

"The show will be up until the end of the month, but I may stay on indefinitely. I haven't decided yet." Bobby looked mildly surprised as Vivian continued, "I'm looking forward to getting to know your daughter. I've told everyone in New York what a curiosity you have in your family."

"I'm glad you find us interesting," Randolph Reeve said with gentle irony.

"An astronomer who's a nun? Now that's original. You must be really proud." All the Reeves were uncomfortable now.

"Miz Reeve, luncheon is served," said the butler, arriving at the door at just the right moment. They followed him into the red dining room. It was the same color as the exhibition room at Bobby's gallery. It had been his inspiration. Chintz curtains boldly printed with amaryllis flowers bristled around the windows, and burnished gold-leaf squares covered the ceiling. The satinwood sideboard groaned under the weight of the family coin silver.

Vivian didn't notice how stilted the conversation was during lunch; in her own eyes, she was charming the senior Reeves with tales of her successes and impressing Bobby and Debo with her savoir-faire. By the time dessert arrived, Bobby was disenchanted. The chocolate soufflé was served to Vivian by white-gloved hands, and in helping herself, she dropped a large spoonful on her lap.

"Oh, hell," she slurred.

Bobby stood up and turned to his parents, "Mom. Dad. Vivian and I hate to leave in the middle of dessert, but we are late for an appointment downtown. Please excuse us." He pulled out Vivian's chair, and as she stood, the blob of soufflé fell onto the silk Persian carpet. Vivian pretended not to notice. The others had.

"Oh, that appointment," Vivian smiled brightly at Bobby. "Judge and Mrs. Reeve, you've got quite some place here. I really enjoyed it."

Bobby steered her out of the house and hustled her into his silver Porsche, relieved, once he got her to the Soniat House, he might not have to see her again that day. Too bad this little hotel was only two blocks from his gallery and three blocks from his apartment. He wished he'd remembered not to get sexually involved with someone he did not know well. Debo had always warned him about that.

Judge Reeve cleared his throat, "Just another egomaniac with low self-esteem."

"Oh, don't take it personally, Daddy. She'd had too much to drink and lost her grip."

"Seems like she lost her grip on Bobby too," Millicent Reeve said, inspecting her manicure.

"Bobby can take care of himself, Mother. You don't ever have to worry about that. Anyway, I have you two alone, at last." While still sitting at the dining room table, Debo told her parents about Lila's accident and how Maria Sanchez was out of work, relying on charity and homesick for Mexico.

It didn't take long for her mother to come up with something. "I could pay for Maria's airfare home and make a contribution to the Jehovah's Witnesses. They do good work, I'm sure." Debo had never doubted her mother's generosity.

As Judge Reeve stirred sugar into his demitasse cup, he said, "Millicent, don't encourage these people. They go around bothering everyone on Saturdays."

"Randolph Reeve, if buying a few Bibles bothers you, you should be ashamed of yourself."

"No more *shaming* or *shoulding*, Millicent."

"Randolph, you've just got to stop reading those psychology books, or you'll be downright certifiable. Why can't we *shame* and *should?* Of all people on the face of this earth, you know that there're things that are just plain shameful and things that should and should not be. You weren't a judge for most of your life to now go and lose contact with the common sense God gave you. I wish you'd stop looking for that inner child and find out where that inner adult went."

Debo loved her parents, her plain-speaking, big-hearted mother and her scholarly father. But her father had changed since his open-heart surgery last year. Physically, he was healthy, but the former take-charge man had disappeared, and this new, timid man now inhabited his body. Debo loved both incarnations of her father. She thought of this change as getting to know his other side.

Her mother was less sure about this other side. She missed his opinions. She missed their arguments. She missed his forcefulness. He still looked the same, tall and strong, but something within him was diminished. Yet she still hoped her old Randolph would be back someday. The way he was. The way she remembered him.

"Aunt May, how do I look?" Angie stood in front of an old-fashioned mahogany looking glass, getting the full-length view of herself. She knew she had never looked better in her life.

"Darlin', you look like the Queen of Sheba! I'm so glad to see those eyes of yours shining again. I want you to have the best time tonight. I want you to dance. I want you to sing. I want you to fall in love again."

Angie reminded herself to slow down and not let the butterflies in her stomach get the better of her. But it wasn't easy. The thrill of being young and beautiful with a handsome man coming to her door at any second was delightful. Her fuchsia silk dress skimmed her thighs, showing off her lovely legs in their gold high-heeled sandals.

The doorbell rang. There stood Sam dressed in a dark blue suit and a starched white shirt. "Sam, come in and meet the most important person in my life."

"Sam, it is certainly good to meet you. I know your parents and your grandparents on both sides." May clasped both of his hands in hers, smiling up at him.

"Ms. Jones, it is an honor for me to meet you. I've heard a lot about you this weekend."

"Well, Angie's my baby. So you be sure to treat her right, now, you hear?"

"Oh, I will. You don't have to worry about that."

Aunt May saw them to the door, and once it had closed, Sam took Angie in his arms and kissed her.

"I made a reservation at the Blue Room. I hope you like it."

"Wonderful, Sam! I love it, and I haven't been there in ages." Angie hoped that she would not know any members of the band. She did not want to be provoked into singing tonight. Tonight, she just wanted to listen to the sound of Sam's voice.

Sam had ordered a bottle of Moet & Chandon, which was already cooling on the table when they arrived. The room looked just like she remembered it, with beautiful blue carpeting and upholstery and crystal chandeliers. She tried to see who was playing in the band, but a column obscured her view.

As the waiter poured the champagne into Sam's glass for him to taste, Angie thought, *Everything's as it should be.*

"To the most beautiful woman in Louisiana," Sam said, raising his glass. After the meal, the two of them danced late into the night and were almost the last to leave. Angie's friend Pete was playing the saxophone. He gave her a wink, sensing tonight was Angie's night for romance, not for singing the blues.

When Angie got home, she changed into her white eyelet pajamas, went into Aunt May's room, and climbed into the big bed, just as she had done so many times as a little girl. "Aunt May, Sam is a fine man, and I'm falling in love with him."

"Oh, baby, I'm so happy." They hugged each other and fell asleep hand in hand.

CHAPTER

9

Early on Labor Day, Lila awoke with a scream in her throat. Her hair was drenched with sweat. She switched on the light, and the nightmare drained out of her, like water swirling down a drain, but sleep eluded her as she thought of the accident and how a nanosecond had separated her from killing this woman. She bit down hard on her lip. The salty, coppery taste of blood jolted her, and she thought of a rosary she had won in a spelling bee in sixth grade, which she had kept all these years in the top drawer of her old wicker desk. She dug it out, climbed back into bed, and began to say the half-remembered prayers. The repetition of the words soothing her, she fell into a deep sleep.

The storm had cleared the air, and a few hours later, the sun was blasting into her room. Seeing the rosary on the bed brought the nightmare vividly back to her mind. She shivered at the thought of nearly killing Maria and of having to drive again, but the twins needed her attention, and the morning passed into afternoon, her thoughts ping-ponging between Maria and Philip.

So what if Philip stopped drinking and drugging for a month? Would that make up for years of uncertainty and the last six months of fear and violence? Memories floated to the surface of her brain. Philip out of control, breaking, kicking, yelling. She felt fear tense the muscles in the small of her back.

Guessing that despite it all, Lila hated the idea of divorce, Ricky Wheeler had not encouraged her to start proceedings. He himself could not take the case due to his close friendship with both Philip and Lila but had not yet suggested another lawyer. What he told her was,

"Take a trip and give yourself a chance to think." Obviously, Ricky did not have children.

Talking though her problems with her friends and family had been helpful to Lila. It had helped straighten out her own mind and had given her a perspective she didn't have before when it was all rattling around randomly in her brain. Even so, she was still uncertain of what it was exactly that she wanted.

At least, Philip was in professional hands now, and she had several weeks to think before seeing him again. Feeling abandoned and resentful that he had not been the husband she expected him to be, she was definitely feeling sorry for herself when the phone rang. It was Debo, who was still at her parents' house, asking her to come over.

"I was just thinking about you. I'll be right there." Lila got into her mother's car and set off down St. Charles Avenue, breathing hard as she passed the raised cottage with the red shutters. *I can do this*, she reminded herself as she continued cautiously to the Reeve's. Life rushes on. *I was lucky.*

The Reeve's living room was Lila's idea of grandeur at its best. The walls were glazed the color of unsalted butter, and lush silk damask curtains of the same shade pooled onto the floor. A portrait of Mrs. Reeve with Bobby and Debo, painted twenty-five years ago hung over the fireplace, the other paintings a mix of nineteenth century Parisian street scenes and paintings bought from Bobby's living artist exhibitions.

After a noisy canine welcome, Lila sank into the pale blue, down-filled sofa, glad that her first car journey was over. She told Debo about her nightmare and how relieved she was that Maria was alive and well. Mrs. Reeve poked her head in to say hello, "Lila, please stay for supper. We're having Gumbo, and Debo doesn't have to be back at the convent until nine."

Debo was comfortably curled up in a yellow silk armchair. She sensed there was something bothering her friend. "Lila, tell me what's on your mind."

"Guess what? I still don't know what to do about Philip. The senior partner at his firm called on Saturday to say they've sent him to a rehab near L.A. I had no idea that his partners knew anything about his drinking. I wonder what he did and how he reacted when they suggested rehab. I couldn't ask Mr. Hardy, but I guess I'll find out eventually. Anyway, I'm supposed to go out there to see him soon, and I'm not sure I ever want to see him again. But there's no one else. With both parents dead and no siblings, there's just me."

"If you ask yourself, 'What is the best, most loving thing I can do?' You will know the answer. This always works for me."

"I thought you had to ask God."

"Sometimes, I don't have time." Debo uncurled and perched on the edge of the deep chair, concentrating on her friend. "Go on. I'm listening."

"It's been hell living with Philip for a long time now. He's a monster when he's drinking. Like Dr. Jekyll and Mr. Hyde. Angie's pastor asked me what I loved about him, and I had to make a real effort to remember any goodness at all. I did remember though. But it seems so long ago."

"How did that make you feel?"

"Sad."

"What about the twins?"

"They're much happier here. They've only asked about him a couple of times."

"What did you say?"

"Oh, I was vague and changed the subject."

"What's the best, most loving thing you can do in this situation?"

"Go to L.A. with an open mind, right?"

"There you go. God doesn't make it hard for us to know his will. You know, we have to obey the law of gravity, but there are other laws, just as immutable, which we can choose to ignore. Like the law of love. But when we obey this law, things go better for us."

"Just because I go out there doesn't mean that all is forgiven and forgotten." Lila was snapping her sandal against her heel. "I didn't marry a drunk drug addict. Philip started all this alcohol and drug abuse, knowing full-well he was married with children."

"Lila, you realize Philip's genes set him up for all this. They must know what they are doing at the rehab. They'll teach him how to reconstruct his life."

"That's the problem. Philip thinks he knows everything already. Youngest partner in the firm, Harvard Law Review, expert on corporate law, et cetera. He's become so arrogant. I don't even know him anymore."

"Mother Fitzpatrick once told me a good definition of humility is the willingness to become and remain teachable."

"Maybe she should tell Philip that. But believe me, he has zero interest in humility."

"God has his part to play too, Lila. You don't have to have all the answers. You know your next step is just to go out there with an open mind. That's all you have to do, and let God be God."

Lila was not so sure. In the last week, she had talked to Angie, Debo, Pastor Jim, Ricky Wheeler, and her parents. Each time, she had felt clearer, but each time, the confusion had come back. Easy for Debo to say, "Let God be God." But what could God do?

"You know, Lila, you don't have to know anything about the electromagnetic field to turn on the lights. It may be a mystery to you, but the lights come on when you flip the switch. You don't even have to believe there *is* an electromagnetic field to use electricity. Why don't you just try prayer and see what happens." Debo relaxed back into the chair.

"Debo, you amaze me, and I hear what you're saying. After I woke up from the nightmare about Maria, I tried the rosary and fell asleep halfway through. I do still know a few prayers by heart and can follow the service with the best of Catholics and Episcopalians, but other than that—"

"Well, you can start by getting on your knees." Lila rolled her eyes dramatically. But Debo continued, "Your brain is very attentive and will notice that you're in an unusual physical position, and it will ask itself, 'What is this woman up to now?' It will be aware that something different is happening. Kneeling is for us, not for God. When you put your hands together, it closes your circuits, so to speak."

"Then what?"

"I usually say a prayer I know by heart because the rhythm of it gets me in the mood. When possible, I like to whisper to get my breath into it. I thank God for some blessings and then concentrate on what I need from him. Sometimes, it's a healing for someone else or guidance for myself, but it can be anything. Anything, Lila."

"Is that all?"

"Personally, I end my prayer thanking Him for taking care of it and praying that His will be done on Earth as it is in heaven. I used to think that God's will was something burdensome. 'Thy will be done' sounded like drudgery to me. But if you think about the whole phrase, you are, in fact, praying for something heavenly."

Long shadows were claiming the room when Judge Reeve came in and turned on the lights. "What're you girls plotting here in the dark?"

"Oh, Daddy, you remember Lila."

"I certainly do, and I'm so glad to see her back in New Orleans! Welcome home, Lila! You're looking prettier than ever!"

"Thank you, Judge! I'm glad to be back!"

Just then, Bobby walked in the door. Lila blushed. "Well, look who's here! Glad to see you, Lila!" His wide grin underlined his words.

The five of them had dinner on a glassed-in porch at the back of the house. The sun was rich and heavy, wantonly spilling its gold onto the gazebo. Lila found herself glancing over at Bobby throughout the meal. He still had that teasing look in his eye and that easy smile she remembered from childhood. Even after all these years, there was something about him she just couldn't resist.

As Lila was driving Debo back to the convent, Debo said, "If I were you, I would pay no attention at all to Bobby. He's such a flirt."

"I wasn't paying any attention to Bobby."

"I was just thinking, if he calls you, don't go out with him or anything until you know what's going on with your marriage."

Lila sighed and said good night to Debo. On the drive uptown, she said, "Damn" out loud to the empty car. *Both times Bobby Reeve ever noticed me, either Angie or Debo was there to observe and comment.*

CHAPTER

10

A week later, Philip was feeling better physically than he had in years. Now that the medication had worn off, he could think clearly and started experiencing surges of optimism. They came like flashes of light, on and off. He liked Peyton, his personal counselor, an intelligent guy in his late thirties who had been clean and sober for five years. They met four times a week, and Philip looked forward to their sessions.

The daily routine at Anderson was well designed, and there was little time for boredom.

Philip liked doing the homework exercises and began to see a pattern in his drug and alcohol abuse through the time line and the personal history that he was working on at Peyton's suggestion. The pattern became clearer and clearer, showing that from an early age his drinking had not been normal. Even thought he was enjoying doing this written work, he was not ready to see the evidence staring him in the face.

In his primary group, there were seven other men and women from diverse backgrounds, but they shared a common problem and could relate to each other on a gut level. Philip was comfortable with these people and liked hearing their stories. Craig was a good roommate, though he would be leaving the men's unit and moving on to extended care soon. Philip was going to miss his wry sense of humor, but they would still see each other at meals.

Explaining that addiction is a disease that affects the mind, body, and spirit, Peyton suggested that Philip think about his concept of a higher power. Philip said, "Sorry, you've got the wrong guy. I was brought up an Episcopalian in a Catholic city. I know all about religion, and I am not interested."

Peyton replied, "They say that religion is for people who are afraid to go to hell, and spirituality is for people who have already been there. We're not trying to promote any organized religion here. We just want you to recognize that *you* didn't create the universe, that *you* aren't the center of it. I suggest you think of something outside yourself that you acknowledge to be greater than yourself and rely on that, call it whatever you want."

"I rely on myself."

"Have you ever tried to stop drinking or using coke on your own?"

"Well, I did, but it was a half-hearted try."

"So you think your willpower alone can regulate your drug and alcohol use?"

"Of course."

"Philip, you're lying to yourself."

"What?" Philip was not accustomed to being challenged, especially about his character.

"You're lying to yourself," Peyton repeated. "Something or a series of somethings happened that were so bad that your wife left you and now your firm decided to send you to Anderson. As a husband and a lawyer, you decided not to use this willpower of yours to avoid this? I want to get this straight. You allowed things to deteriorate to the point that your wife left and your firm intervened rather than try harder?" Peyton's jaw tightened.

"It wasn't that bad. What I did, I did on my own time."

"I wonder why they sent you here then?"

"They're just overreacting."

"They had a hired hand fly with you all the way from Tokyo, and things weren't so bad?"

"Look. I've no idea why they sent me here other than I was a little drunk a couple of times. And they all drink. My colleagues drink. My clients drink. It's the world I live in. And as for cocaine, I only use it on social occasions."

"Most people never use cocaine on any occasion, Philip."

"Listen, you sanctimonious bastard, you sit here in this fancy rehab and have no idea what it is like in the real world."

"Would you hire a lawyer who drinks and drugs the way you do?"

"Of course. I do a great job. My clients love me."

"Why do you think your firm singled you out for rehab then? Or do they send all of their lawyers to rehab?"

For a moment, Philip stopped to think. As far as he knew, he was the only one Asher, Clarke had sent to rehab so far. With seven hundred lawyers worldwide, he could not be sure, but offhand, he could not think of anyone else.

Then explaining that denial is a symptom of the disease, Peyton said that most addicts think that the alternate reality produced by mood-altering substances is the true one, revealing their real selves. Philip laughed and said, "Not applicable to me! It just makes me more myself."

"Exactly," was all Peyton said.

"Okay, maybe people from New Orleans drink a little harder than others. Maybe I like to drink more than most, but I can handle it. I've learned a lot here this week, and I can cut back. That won't be a problem."

"You're free to go any time, Philip. If you don't think you belong here, you're wasting my time, your firm's money, and your life."

"What do you mean 'wasting my life'?"

"You're an alcoholic and an addict. If you think that is how you want to live your life, then it's wasted. Remember, this is an incurable, progressive, and fatal disease. It gets worse over time."

"I'm a good provider for my family. No one could ever deny that."

"I talked to your wife just yesterday, and it seems you kicked a chair your four-year-old was standing on, which resulted in a serious head injury."

"I don't remember doing that." Philip looked carefully at his shoes.

"So it's okay to do it as long as you don't remember it?"

"I didn't say that. He shouldn't have been standing on the chair."

"He's four years old, Philip. Four-year-olds sometimes stand on chairs, and most fathers don't then kick the chair."

"Look, I didn't mean to hurt him."

"Your wife said it was bad."

"These things won't happen again."

"Good. Well, our time's up now. I would like you to try and remember kicking that chair. If you can, please write down what your feelings were preceding the violence. See you Monday."

Philip considered punching Peyton but got up and shook his hand, "Okay, see you Monday."

CHAPTER

11

Since he had dropped Philip off at Anderson, Ned Kirby had been working hard. Not only had he arranged for elocution lessons for his time in L.A., but he went straight to work putting another, more urgent plan into action.

For over two years, he and Philip had been working together on an acquisition for their client, Pan Asian Cable Communications, a publically held Japanese company. Golden Harvest Group, a private Hong Kong based company that manufactures fiber optics and coaxial cable, was the company being acquired.

The final draft was ready for the closing, scheduled the following week. Philip's absence at the signing would be a surprise to the president of Pan Asian, but Hardy decided not to tell him in advance. It was agreed that nothing needed to be said other than that there was a family emergency.

Ned was counting on the fact that only Robert Hardy, Philip, and himself could make changes to the acquisition document online, using a code name and a private six to ten digit number. Pan Asian was buying Golden Harvest Group for four billion Hong Kong dollars, 500 million U.S. The success fee for this would be 25 million U.S. dollars for Asher, Clarke. This was a big deal for the firm and Ned well knew it.

Sitting poolside that first day at the Beverly Wilshire, Ned hacked into the firm's computer and scrolled down to where he needed to make the changes. He was confident this would be safe as it was the middle of the night in Tokyo. The only danger would be if Hardy or Philip were accessing the document at the same time. Since Hardy was in Tokyo and Philip was in rehab, he figured he could take his time. He smiled as he worked, thinking that if the client ever saw this doctored document, Asher, Clarke would lose face in Asia forever. He wasn't worried that they would actually see it though.

The changes would take less than thirty minutes, but there was the matter of Philip's access number. Ned knew Philip's code name from the beginning. That was no secret. It was important for the three of them to know who had made which additions to the document and when. The number was the problem. Banking on Philip's using his birthday or his wife's or the twin's, Ned had that information with him. None of these worked. He tried the family phone numbers. No luck. Then he tried all of these numbers in reverse. Finally, Lila's international cell number in reverse gave him the opportunity to sign in as Phillip. The log, if they could ever reaccess it, would read that Philip made the changes from his laptop five hours after checking into Anderson.

After setting his plan into motion, Ned relaxed into a few days of shopping, voice lessons, and high living in L.A. Since he was there, he took advantage of unused vacation time.

Landing in Tokyo at dawn on Friday, Ned went straight to the office. In the building's gym, he showered, shaved, and put on the Ermenegildo Zegna suit he had purchased on Rodeo Drive. He then went up to his office and printed out the document and called Robert Hardy on his cell. "Mr. Hardy, this is Ned Kirby, and I would like to see you as soon as possible."

Hardy noticed the new Hollywood accent right away and smiled. "I'm on my way in right now. I'll be there in about twenty minutes. Come to my office. I'm looking forward to hearing about Philip."

"Yes, sir. I want to talk to you about him."

Ned brought the document with him, marked with red tabs at the twelve pertinent places.

"Mr. Hardy, this document has been signed off on, but I thought I'd check it. There are a few pages you need to see."

Putting on his reading glasses and looking over the passages Ned had marked, Hardy's dark blue eyes narrowed. He looked up at Ned and said, "Thank you for bringing this to my attention. How was your trip to L.A.?" Ned couldn't believe it, but Hardy sounded calm.

"Well, I got Philip to the rehab, and I spent my vacation time there with old friends. It was great." Ned was lying. The only person he knew there was his voice coach.

"That will be all for now, Ned. I'll get back to you on this." Hardy pointed to the thick document lying on his desk.

Adrenalin racing, Hardy called Fred Brewster, the head of Asher, Clarke Asia. Brewster was in Singapore on business, but promised he would be in Hardy's office first thing on Monday.

Hardy had breakfast laid out in the small soundproof room off his office and pointed out to Brewster the places marked by Ned. There was silence as Brewster calculated the cost to the firm. "What does the log show? When was the document last accessed?"

"Can't tell. The log was wiped clean. Unfortunately, our computer guy's in Manila and not due back until Thursday."

"Who could've done this?" Brewster asked.

"Anyone who wants to make Asher, Clarke the laughing stock of Asia. Or possibly Golden Harvest doesn't really want to sell. Or

Pan Asian doesn't really want to buy." Hardy looked exhausted.

"How did you catch it?"

"Kirby brought it to my attention."

"Can you think of any reason why Philip Williams would want to sabotage the firm?"

"It's not like him, but to make sure, I had every case he has worked on in the last six months brought to my office. I looked over everything this weekend. Nothing else's amiss. He could be on someone else's payroll, but it's hard to believe, or maybe he did it just because he was angry we sent him to rehab. Or maybe he was drunk. Who knows?" Hardy rubbed his temples.

"We can't take any chances. We'd better have a look at his calendar and see what company he has been keeping lately." Fred Brewster picked up a paper clip lying on the table and straightened it.

"I've already checked his calendar. Nothing."

"The closing has to take place tomorrow. We can investigate this later."

"Agreed. I'm going to have these errors corrected and the document printed out. Then, Fred, you and I are going over all two hundred and

twelve pages together before I put it in the safe."
Hardy stood, and the meeting was adjourned.

———◆———

That same Monday, Philip came to his appointment with Peyton in a better mood. He wanted
to thank Peyton for his time and tell him that
he would be leaving. He decided he was not an
alcoholic. His mother had been an alcoholic,
and she had died before she was his age. And his
drinking was not like hers. He was confident he
could drink moderately, and he had decided to
give up cocaine. "I'm sorry I called you a bastard,
Peyton."

"It's okay. I've been called worse."

"I know you are trying to get me to see that
I can't manage my drinking, but I can. And I'm
going to give up cocaine. That's the problem."

"Look, Philip, sorry to interrupt you, but you
have to call your office right away."

The look of confidence fell from Philip's face.
"Who called?"

"I don't know. I just got a message that it's
urgent for you to call. There's a phone room

across from the reception desk. Whoever's at the desk will put the call through for you."

Philip calculated the time change. It was now 7:00 a.m. Tuesday morning in Tokyo. He gave Ned's cell number to the receptionist and waited in the small room.

Ned had been celebrating his victory over Philip all weekend and was still feeling the effects when the call came through.

"Ned, Buddy! This is Philip. I got a message to call the office. Do you know what this is about? Hope everything's okay with the Pan Asian closing."

"I haven't heard anything. The closing's this morning. How're you doing?"

"There's nothing wrong with me. I'll be back soon."

When the called ended, Philip sat back in the chair and stared at the phone. He did not know whether to call Hardy or Brewster. Brewster was his direct boss, but he knew Hardy liked him better. After a few moments, he gave the receptionist another number.

"Brewster," a brusque voice answered.

"Fred, this is Philip Williams."

"Oh, Philip. There were some irregularities concerning the currency in the closing document. We need some time to sort this out. Why don't you stay where you are for a couple of months?"

Philip turned bright red. "You'll have to be more specific. I don't know what you are talking about."

"Sorry, Philip, but I need more information before I talk to you about this. You just work on your problem, and we'll work on ours. Talk to you soon." The connection was cut.

Philip slumped forward on the metal desk, his head in his hands.

Once Philip pulled himself together, he headed back to his counselor's office. "Hey, Peyton. I feel like a man without a country. Something's up in Japan, and I'm *persona non grata* there. Lila's at her parents' with the twins. So I guess I'm stuck here with you.

"Take a seat. Let's talk."

Philip explained his role in the Pan Asian deal and the two brief phone calls. "It beats me what could've happened. The documents had been signed-off on before I left Tokyo."

"You could've done something in a blackout."

"I can't be sure, can I? You've got my attention now, and I'm going to stay the course here. Funny. Less than an hour ago, I was coming to tell you, 'my bags are packed, and I'm outta here.'"

"There's nothing you can do about the past, Philip, but you can change the going forward. Let's hope you get your priorities in order while you're here."

Philip's eyes widened slightly. In a flash, he saw the moral squalor in his life, recognizing the pollution of addiction had separated him by light-years from his original values.

"You haven't talked about how your mother's alcoholism affected you as a child. Can you remember specific incidents?"

"Not really. Let's not go back there."

Philip's first memory was of being awakened by his mother wearing a rubber full-face mask of a witch, hairy warts included. He began to scream. His mother picked him up instinctively, but her voice, distorted by the mask, terrified him and his screams intensified. His father came into the room and ripped the mask off his wife. Philip fainted. He did not remember how old he was, but he was still sleeping in a crib. Other memories included being so frightened by her drunk driving that he often climbed into the backseat and pressed himself flat on the floor. Once, she forgot he was in the car and left him for several hours lying there on the floor of her car, abandoned in the street outside a tavern.

He remembered her as being a pretty petite brunette, sweet and shy when sober and alternately nasty and embarrassingly affectionate when drunk. At an early age, Philip retreated to his room and closed the door, rarely seeking out either of his parents. After his mother's death, he and his father were formally polite to each other, but there was never any intimacy. But he loved his parents despite it all and, loyally, never spoke of his childhood. Was this good or bad? He didn't know or care. It was just that way for him and being in rehab with a personal counselor was not going to change that.

A few hours later in Tokyo, the closing took place in the large boardroom at Asher, Clarke. Two of the walls were glass, two were cream-colored lacquer, hung with contemporary Japanese paintings. At the bleached oak table, clients and lawyers were seated in exact order of protocol. The swivel armchairs were covered in soft leather the same shade as the table. In front of each place was a copy of the document, white thermos of ice water, cut crystal glass, and stainless steel felt pen with Asher, Clarke Asia in bold burgundy lettering.

Philip's not being at the table was disappointing to the president of Pan Asian who was ready with an 18k gold Dunhill pen. It is traditional for a Japanese businessman to give a handsome present at a closing, though an assistant usually presents it. In this case, it was more than just tradition; he genuinely liked Philip and told Hardy he wanted to present the gift himself. The fact that this was a high compliment to Philip was not lost on Hardy.

The closing went as planned, with Ned using his newly acquired accent. But inside, he was nervous. How had the firm dealt with Philip? Was his plan working?

CHAPTER

12

The twins started Trinity, their new kindergarten, the Wednesday after Labor Day. This left Lila free from 8:30 to 11:30 on weekdays. After getting them settled, she thought she would take Debo's advice and try prayer.

She went into the dark church, got on her knees, and said the Lord's Prayer. She felt comforted by the rhythm of it, as Debo had said. She said it silently once and whispered it once and thanked God that she had not killed Maria. Her stomach churned for a moment. Then, she thanked God for her healthy children, for her parents, for Angie and Debo. She asked for wisdom and guidance about what to do with her marriage and thanked God for dealing with it.

Well, that wasn't so hard, she thought to herself. Going back to the car she wondered what to do next and decided to drive to the Levee and walk along it.

There was a lot of activity on the river. Voices of seamen as they called to each other, the smell of the Mississippi River mud, cries of gulls circling overhead lulled her anxious mind. She was alert to everything going on around her and breathed deeply. Her shoes were pinching her toes. Tomorrow, she would wear sneakers. She was aware of being part of this vibrant scene and walked for almost an hour, ignoring her toes.

Then she drove to the Café du Monde for coffee and donuts, enjoying her time alone. The chicory coffee was hot and strong; the donuts melted in her mouth. Soon, it would be time to pick up the twins. She thought she would take them to lunch at the Camellia Grill and to Paul's Sno-ball stand for bubblegum Sno-balls for dessert. She knew they would love the technicolor effect produced by eating this ice. She remembered being so proud of having a blue tongue, blue teeth, blue gums. She loved the adults pretending to be worried about the symptoms, saying that a specialist must be found for the blue-mouthed children.

She drove uptown to the corner of Jackson and Coliseum, parked, and waited until she saw the children tumbling out of the classroom. She scooped them up in her arms and asked them to explain to her exactly what it was like to be a kindergarten student at Trinity. She had gone there herself but could barely remember. The most exciting thing was Pepper, a service dog, who had come to school that day. He was a big black Lab who liked being read to aloud. They told her when they learned to read well enough, they would read to Pepper. They agreed that *Good Night Moon* would be his kind of book.

After lunch, Sno-balls were consumed, resulting in the astonishing blueness. The Parkers had not forgotten their roles and mocked horror at what had happened to Lila and the twins.

That week and the next, the days blended into each other, and after dropping off the twins, Lila established the routine of praying and walking on the Levee. By Friday, she felt like she had done this for months. Getting more comfortable in the church, more comfortable with her prayers, she thought how odd it was that in ten days, the practice seemed second nature to her. She was looking forward to telling Debo this the next day over lunch.

The two friends met at Manale's for oysters. It was just around the corner from the convent and was as comfortable as an old shoe. Coming in out of the glaring sun into the cool, dark, old-fashioned interior was a relief. The savory smell of garlic and briny oysters was a balm to them both. The waiter brought a basket of garlic bread to the table and took their drink orders.

"You know, I'm leaving for L.A. next Sunday, Debo. I'm not dreading it anymore, but I still think it'll be awkward."

"You don't have to worry. You can be sure that God is in this with you. Your part is to do the best, most loving thing for all concerned, including yourself. I've been praying for you to have clarity in this."

"I don't know if I have clarity exactly, but I do have a calmness that I didn't have last week. And

I have been praying. Simply. Like you described. It feels natural now."

"It is natural, Lila. As natural and nourishing as breathing." Debo brushed garlic breadcrumbs off her black shirt.

"Why do these things happen to us? Why'd Angie lose her family like that? Why's Philip an addict? And what about me? I practically killed Maria."

"First of all, you didn't 'practically kill' Maria. Think about it. Some good will actually come from all this. My mother has gotten in touch with her. They're going to meet at the convent on Thursday morning at ten. The twins will be in school, so you can come too."

"Maybe seeing her will stop the nightmares and turn this whole thing around."

After they had ordered their oysters, Debo took a sip of her ginger ale. "We all ask why there are tragedies in life. A yoga teacher in Boston once told me that being here, on Earth, we're partially separated from God, which makes us uncomfortable. He said being here is like being in reform school for the soul. Some have lighter sentences than others, but we all have lessons to learn, and

God doesn't intervene, unless asked. He said each of us has times of learning and times of teaching. He said our souls have chosen this life for its lessons. Anyhow, it meant something to me. I don't know if it makes any sense to you."

"It does, actually. I remember being three years old. My grandmother had just died. Seeing my mother cry frightened me so much that I hid from her underneath a skirted table in the hall. I remember *knowing* that I had seen something like a movie of this life and that I had chosen it or agreed to it somehow. I felt everything would be okay. I wasn't alone. That was just before my sister was born, and I really was a lone child in a house full of grief. Strange, but that's what I remember."

"Children are more aware of other dimensions than adults are. I'm a firm believer in that."

"Did you talk to your colleagues at NASA like this?"

"Lila, I dated my colleagues. There was no opportunity for such discussions."

"Oh, Debo."

Debo was still in class teaching when Mrs. Reeve and Lila met Maria in the visitor's room at the convent. She was a slim woman in her late forties, wearing glasses, hair pulled back in a bun. Lila thought to herself, *I put those crutches in her hands. I put that Kevlar boot on her foot.* Maria sloughed off their inquires about her leg but answered their questions about her family readily. Lila and Mrs. Reeve found out all about her four children and seven grandchildren in Mexico City. Mrs. Reeve promised to drive her to the airport and see her off. Later that afternoon, Lila and Mrs. Reeve went shopping and bought two suitcases and clothes and toys to fill them.

As it turned out Maria's journey back home to Mexico City was the day Lila left for L.A. Lila was restless on the flight and felt a flutter of fear as she disembarked. She hugged her cotton sweater around her as she followed the signs to baggage claim. Once she spotted the driver from Anderson behind the glass partition holding the sign with her name on it, she felt a sense of purpose. Waving to him, she reminded herself she was here to do her part with an open mind.

She was driven to a nearby motel where she would be staying for five days with family members of other Anderson clients. This motel was by no means luxurious, but there was a pool in the courtyard behind the reception area. Groups of people sat around it, colorful drinks with umbrellas and straws on tables in front of them. She imagined herself there, reading a good book through large sunglasses, with nothing to do but wallow in the dazzling afternoon. She walked down the corridor to her no-frills room, showered, and unpacked. Despite her conflicting thoughts, one minute wanting to be supportive of Philip, the next wanting to abandon him, she dressed and was ready to go in a van with other family members for the 5:00 p.m. orientation meeting.

In all, there were about fifteen family members gathered in the room designated to be their base for the week ahead. That first evening, they met Peyton and the other counselors and were given reading material and a map of the center. A clinical psychologist talked to them about the importance of going to Al-Anon meetings. She explained that Al-Anon is a support group for the families of addicts and attending these meetings would help them learn how to take care of themselves. Their own experiences, she said, could be helpful to another person and getting to know others in the group would ensure knowing someone to call if there were any difficulties. She added, "If you choose not to go to these meetings, you will not only miss out on the wisdom of the group but will miss the opportunity to help a fellow sufferer." She stressed that family members could not be the cause of addiction nor could they control or cure it. There was a general sigh of relief.

Following this introductory session, everyone moved on to meet their family members. Lila looked at Philip standing there. Her husband, the father of her children was standing there waiting for her greeting. She wanted to push him away and run in the other direction but managed a stiff smile and a peck on the cheek. She shoved her iPhone at him and brought up photos of the twins. This small object, this thin barrier was all she had to put between them, her only protection.

"Philip, are you having any fun yet?" Lila's voice was angry, but not as angry as she suddenly felt. Her raw hostility surprised her. "Does the whole firm know you are here? Is there a job waiting for you when you go back?"

"Lila, I'm not here to have fun. And yes, I think everyone in the Tokyo office probably knows I'm here. As far as I know, I still have a job, and I am very grateful that you made the effort to come here."

"I had no choice in the matter. Who else is there?" Lila recognized the pain in Philip's face and softened her voice. "Of course, I want to be supportive." She thought of Debo. This was not the best, most loving way to handle the situation. The moment had gotten away from her. She wished she could start over.

"Let's go in with the others for dinner."

After serving themselves, they sat with Craig Stein, Philip's first roommate, and his current roommate, Nigel Shaw. Nigel had come from London. He was thirty-nine, six feet tall, with longish curly brown hair. He had too many eyelashes and the gift of making a mockery of everyone and everything without going too far.

Within minutes, he had the whole table howling with laughter, helping to break the ice between Philip and Lila.

After dinner, there was free time before the families were driven back to their motel. Following Nigel to the outdoor smoking area, Philip and Lila watched him try to light a cigar in the wind. "Bloody hell, why does smoking have to be such a challenge in America? I think while I'm out here I should try to find out if there are any truly tolerant, liberal-minded people left in California and start a movement demanding indoor smoking. You could be the lawyer for this group, Philip. What do you say?"

"I think that would be just the sort of thing Asher, Clarke would encourage their partner-on-probation to do."

This was the first Lila had heard of trouble in Tokyo, but she bit her tongue. Her thoughts raced on the treadmill of her mind as she ran through some possibilities. She watched the blue smoke of Nigel's cigar disperse into the night and wondered how all of this would be resolved. What was she doing in southern California with these two strangers? She felt out of place and envious of Philip and Nigel's camaraderie. She longed for Angie and Debo.

Once back at the motel, she changed into her pajamas and opened the Anderson information packet. Finding a yellow highlighter included, she smiled and propped herself up on the pillows, knees bent, and dove right into the material. Ever since first grade, Lila highlighted everything she found surprising, delightful, or wise. She thought this practice made her a good journalist, easily able to identify the meat and deliver it undiluted. Halfway though, eyelids leaden, she switched off the light, not noticing she had forgotten to pray that day.

CHAPTER

13

ila liked the routine for Family Week at Anderson, which included instruction about the disease of addiction, a time for family members to confront their addicts with the instances most harmful to them, and a time for the addicts to air their grievances. All of this happened in front of the group and the counselors. Lila was surprised and comforted to find she related to the feelings of the others in her group.

When it was Lila's turn to tell her story, she described how she had spent the last four years, since the twins were born, full of apprehension, worrying about Philip's mood when he came home. More and more often, he was hostile to her and impatient with the twins, and their sex life was dead. She said how embarrassed she was by his loud and arrogant behavior in public and described Philip's rage, resulting in Charlie's black eye. She recounted the children's questions about their father and her frustration in not having any answers.

Sitting next to her, listening to all of this, Philip was able to say with genuine sincerity how sad he was to have caused her so much pain. He said he regretted not having been a good father or husband and that he hoped that she would give him a second chance. "You know I am sorry. And I know 'sorry' doesn't change things. So the important thing I want to say is that I was wrong, and I am going to take whatever actions necessary to change." They both had tears in their eyes at the end of the session, each feeling compassion for the other. Philip reached instinctively for Lila's hand. "I know it will take time for you to trust me again, but please don't give up on me yet." Lila let her hand lie in Philip's but did not return the pressure.

At dinner that night, Philip told her the little he knew about the investigation going on in Tokyo and mentioned Ned had not returned his repeated phone calls. "All Brewster told me is that there were some irregularities in the closing document. I promise you, Lila, I have a completely clean conscience." He did not mention that it was possible that anything could have happened in a blackout.

"Did he give you any indication what it's about?"

"None. He told me to focus on my problem."

"He must not think you have anything to do with it."

"He did say I should stay here for a couple of months. I don't think that's so good."

The next afternoon, sitting in the family group therapy session, Lila came to understand how her constant avoidance of confrontation with Philip enabled him to continue his drinking and drugging. She recognized that her fear of losing him had made her his willing hostage. Hearing the stories of the other group members gave her a perspective that she could never have come to on her own. She was taken aback by the level of honesty in that hermetically sealed atmosphere, all these people speaking openly about their intimate experiences and fears. This could never have taken place in a therapist's office in such a short time.

Day by day, hour by hour, tears and laughter purged the built-up anger. Meal times were no longer awkward, thanks, in part, to Nigel's sense of humor. Nigel was a week behind Philip in the process, but he was relaxed and confident. This was not his first time in rehab.

By the end of the week, Lila realized that Philip, at least for now, was serious about maintaining his sobriety. It was decided that Philip would return to New Orleans in two weeks to wait out the investigation going on in Tokyo. Where he would stay was not yet clear. There were several halfway houses in New Orleans and plenty of Alcoholic Anonymous and Narcotics Anonymous meetings. Lila would make some inquiries upon her return and take care of the arrangements for him.

Lila got home late Friday night. Anxious to hear about the trip, her mother was waiting up for her. "Lila, tell me how it was."

"Well, Philip seems much more like the man I married now. I'm starting to feel hopeful we'll get back together."

Her mother hugged her and said, "I'm so glad, honey. You have been through hard times, and I just know things will work out for you. By the way, before I forget, Bobby Reeve called you the other day and wants you to call him back."

Lila registered this news in her stomach; a shiver of excitement blasted up her spine. "Good night, darlin' Lila. I won't let the twins wake you before eight." Lila kissed her mother's cheek and said good night.

She closed her door, smiling as she unpacked and got ready for bed. Drifting off to sleep, she called up her childhood fantasy of Bobby.

After a quick breakfast with the twins, Lila called Ricky Wheeler. Ricky suggested that Philip stay with him and added, "I don't keep alcohol in my apartment, and because of my family's crazy drinking, I go to Al-Anon meetings twice a week. You can come with me if you'd like, Lila." She thanked Ricky warmly for his offer to take Philip in, but put off accepting going to meetings with him. "I learned a lot at Anderson, and I don't like to take time away from the twins, but thank you so much, Ricky, for your thoughtfulness." Lila couldn't wait to get Ricky off the phone. It was her next call that was occupying her mind.

She called the number Bobby had left. "Reeve Gallery, good morning."

"Bobby, this is Lila. Mother said you called while I was away."

"Lila! The Vivian Bruns show is over, and the gallery's back to normal. I would love you to see the collection."

"And I would love to see it. Are you open today?"

"We don't open to the public until noon. Why don't you come over now before we open?"

"I can be there about ten-thirty."

"Excellent! I look forward to seeing you then."

Lila felt panicked, guilty, and joyous. She tore off her clothes and jumped into the shower to wash her hair. She felt the excitement flowing over her as intensely as she felt the warm water. While massaging the sweet-smelling shampoo into her hair, she mentally searched her closet. She wanted to look like she had made no effort and, at the same time, be irresistible. Definitely, the Armani blue jeans on the bottom, but what top? As she rinsed out the conditioner, she decided on a plain white cotton T-shirt and flip-flops.

While carefully drying her hair, she squinted down at her toes and changed her mind about the flip-flops. Once her hair was dry, she slipped on a terry cloth robe and went barefoot into her mother's room. "Mother, do you have any blue flats I can borrow?"

"Help yourself, honey," her mother replied. Mrs. Parker was at her desk, buried in paper-work. She did not even look up and just nodded when Lila asked her to keep an eye on the twins while she went out to run some errands.

Lila's hands were really shaking now, and it was difficult to apply her makeup. She sat down, closed her eyes, and forced herself to breathe from her belly for a full three minutes before she could continue. Once the makeup was applied and the rose perfume sprayed, Lila looked at herself in the full-length bathroom mirror. *Not bad*, she thought. *I've still got it.*

It was ten past ten. Time to go. She went into her mother's room again to get her car keys. "Thanks for the shoes! I'll be back after lunch."

Her mother looked up from her desk. "Since you are taking my car, will you pick up some grape juice and graham crackers on your way home? If I think of something else, I'll text you."

"Sure. And thanks for watching the twins." Lila was eager to be on her way.

She drove slowly, breathing rhythmically as the yoga master in Tokyo had taught her. *I must be crazy. Just looking at some paintings, not throwing the Earth out of orbit.*

She parked her car and checked her profile in the window of Bobby's gallery.

Bobby saw this and opened the door before she reached it, locking it behind her. "Lila! Come on in, and tell me what you think!"

The room had been transformed. The nineteenth century Louisiana landscapes looked luminous against the red walls. There was an entirely different atmosphere from the opening night of Vivian's show.

"Oh, Bobby, this is fantastic! It's amazing that this color works so well with the paintings!" She knows she's there to see the paintings, not to marvel at the color of the walls, yet she babbles on, "You know, when Turner willed his estate to the British Nation, he stipulated that his paintings be hung on a red background."

"Well, he certainly knew what he was talking about, didn't he?"

"Amazing, isn't it?" Lila controlled the tone of her voice, camouflaging her electrifying attraction.

Bobby took her arm. "I want to show you my favorite one," he said, walking her over to a Richard Clague landscape on the Mississippi. The shock of his touch made Lila stumble. Bobby increased the pressure on her arm to support her. Sure that Bobby had felt the current pass between them, Lila lifted her face toward him for the long awaited kiss, but her cell phone rang and broke the spell. Automatically, she reached into her bag, cursing herself for not having silenced it, keeping only the scent of him as she turned away to answer.

"Lila! Get home now," shouted her mother. "Charlotte has a temperature of 105 degrees.

I can't believe you didn't notice when you said good-bye!"

"Oh my God! I'm on my way." In her rush to get to Bobby, she hadn't even said good-bye to the twins. Remorse quenched the lust, and her reason took over. She called Angie but only got her voice mail. She looked up at Bobby. "That was my mother. Charlotte has a fever. I have to go." She ran to the door and fumbled with the lock. Looking over her shoulder, she said, "Please call Angie at St. Joseph's. Tell her to come to my house right away."

"Lila, are you all right to drive? Let me take you home."

"No. No, I am all right, just get the message to Angie."

Bobby unlocked the door and helped Lila to her car, which was only a few steps from the gallery. As she drove off, the scene flooded back, and embarrassment was added to her roiling emotions. *Maybe Bobby had no intention of kissing me. Maybe he was just showing me his paintings. If the phone hadn't rung, I would've surely reached for him.* Clamping both hands on the steering wheel, shaking it in frustration, Lila's whole body cringed.

From a block away, Lila could see Angie's car parked in front of her parents' house. She relaxed her grasp on the steering wheel, pulled into the garage, and slammed the car into park. Entering through the kitchen door, she could see Angie calmly stoking Charlotte's head on the sofa in the adjoining room.

Lila's eyes locked on Angie's, trying to decipher the level of her concern, but Angie showed no emotion. "I told Charlotte we would take her to St. Joseph's so she could see where I work. She's going to bring her stuffed giraffe, and we'll go in my car."

Realizing Angie wanted to run some tests, Lila's shoulders tensed as she smiled at Charlotte. "Honey, you just stay here with Gran and Charlie for a minute while Angie and I go find Jeepers."

Once out of earshot, Lila grabbed Angie's arm. "What do you think it is?"

"Probably just a simple febrile seizure, but I want to make sure she doesn't have meningitis. I'm just glad I was here when she had the seizure. Your mother was totally panicked. It only lasted a few seconds. Pack an overnight bag for you and Charlotte. Better stay at St. Joseph's until the tests come back."

Lila nodded and headed upstairs to pack. The word *seizure* frightened her, but she responded quickly to Angie's directions.

On seeing her mother with a suitcase, Charlotte looked distressed. "Don't go away again, Mommy!"

"I thought it would be fun to stay at Angie's hospital tonight! Just you, me, and Angie."

"Where's Jeepers?"

Lila went back upstairs for the giraffe.

St. Joseph's was one of the newest and most highly regarded children's hospitals in the country. The check-in process was swift and simple, and Charlotte found herself in a cheery room with yellow and white striped walls. There was a bed for her and a bed for Lila. "Where's Angie going to sleep?"

"Don't you worry about me, honey girl. I'll have a cot brought in. Now all we need from you is just a few drops of blood. I promise you won't notice."

"Eeeuuu!"

"I only need a tiny bit. You won't feel a thing," coaxed Angie, holding her hand. Angie handed Charlotte two small chewable tablets. "Here. Pop these in your mouth while I take it. They are yummy and will make you feel better."

Lila switched on the TV and motioned Angie toward the door. "Well?"

"I can't be certain until I see the blood report. It could be roseola."

"What the heck is roseola?"

"It's very common, a mild virus. If it's that, she could go home right now, but let's wait and see."

"Is it contagious?"

"If so, Charlie has already been exposed, but if you are worried about her kindergarten class, all of them have been exposed years ago and have either had it themselves or have the antibodies. It's very common in the US."

The blood tests came back negative for meningitis, nothing more than roseola, but the three of them stayed in the hospital for the night. Once Charlotte was sleeping soundly, Lila and Angie had time to talk. "I feel so guilty that I didn't notice this sooner. She seemed fine at breakfast, but I left the house without checking on her."

"Oh, Lila, roseola is not your fault, but feel guilty if you want to."

Lila wondered if she should tell Angie about the almost kiss, but decided not to. "Should I try to get in touch with Philip?"

"This is so mild, I wouldn't alarm him. Let him concentrate on recovering from his own disease."

They left the hospital after breakfast the next day. Charlotte's temperature was almost back to normal, but they decided she would stay home from school until Wednesday.

That Wednesday, Lila got back into her routine of going to church after dropping the twins off and taking her solitary walks along the Levee. After she started doing this again, she felt the calmness return.

In her prayers, she thanked God that both twins were healthy, that Philip was getting better, and that Maria was safely back in Mexico City. She also thanked him that she had not made a fool of herself over Bobby. The physical sensation of gratitude surprised her. She experienced a joyful feeling in the upper part of her chest, which lasted throughout the morning and well into the afternoon.

CHAPTER

14

Ten days later, Ricky Wheeler went with Lila to pick up Philip at the airport. Philip was relaxed and seemed happy to be staying at Ricky's. Ricky gave Philip a schedule for A.A. meetings and told him not to be surprised if he knew a few people there. The Saturday A.A. meeting was in the same location as Ricky's Al-Anon meeting, and they arrived about ten minutes early and went into separate rooms. As Philip walked in the door, he heard a man call his name. He looked around and saw several familiar faces from his school days. One man gestured to come and sit with them and said, "We've been saving a seat for you here, Philip!"

They laughed at the coincidence of being in the same position. Philip had not seen any of these men for five years, and they each had a story to tell about the journey to A.A. This put Philip at ease; he knew he was in the right place, and he was going to give this his best shot.

Both meetings ended at one o'clock, and Ricky and Philip joined some others at PJ's Coffee House for lunch. Philip thought he was an expert on recovery until he started talking to his friends. He realized that he had just begun and that there was much more ahead. All of these men said they went to meetings to remind themselves what it was like before they got sober and to help a newcomer like himself. They gave him their cell phone numbers and encouraged him to call them any time, day or night. Ricky suggested that Philip listen carefully at meetings and choose a sponsor who would help him through the 12 Steps. Even though this was exactly what had been told to him at Anderson, in the back of Philip's mind, he thought he was above A.A. He had told Peyton that he could do this sobriety thing alone. He remembered Peyton had replied, "Maybe. But you don't have to." Now he was changing his mind about A.A. He was even beginning to see his part in situations, which he had previously blamed on others.

That afternoon, Philip went to the Parkers to see Charlie and Charlotte for the first time in over six weeks. They were waiting quietly, sitting on the floor in the hall trying to play jacks. Lila sensed they were uncomfortable, hovering over them when the doorbell rang. They jumped up and ran to Philip, each one grabbing a leg, but Lila noticed their reticence. Philip did not appear to be aware of this and brought out two books, settled into an armchair in the living room and began reading to them. During the first book, the twins were sitting on the sofa opposite him, but during the second, they climbed onto his lap, responding to the change in him. Lila thought about what Debo had said. *Do children really have a heightened perception?* she wondered.

Robert Hardy was back in New York and called to explain what was happening in Tokyo. He told Philip how the final document read when Ned brought it to his attention. The computer log had been retrieved, and it showed that the changes had come from Philip's laptop several hours after he arrived at Anderson. The implication that Philip was out to get revenge for being sent away outraged Philip who protested his innocence, pointing out that his computer was under lock and key at the time. Hardy calmed him down and said there was evidence of tampering. He said he would check with Anderson to see if they had a receipt for the computer. The investigation was not over, and more would be known next week. The computer-programming expert was working on it. Philip detected a slight chill in Hardy's voice.

While all of this was happening, Philip got news from Craig Stein who was still in the extended care unit at Anderson that Nigel Shaw had gone back to London. When Nigel arrived, the Rolls met him at Heathrow, and his girl-friend was in the backseat with iced champagne and an ounce of coke. He died of an accidental overdose six days later. This news shook Philip to the core.

Lila was beginning to feel guilty that she had not gone with Ricky to Al-Anon meetings. She kept remembering a quote she heard at Anderson, something like "Contempt, prior to investigation, will keep a person in eternal ignorance." Certainly food for thought.

Since Philip's return, he came to the Parker's house every day at four-thirty, took the twins for a walk, and read to them before dinner. Cheerful now, he usually stayed on to chat with Lila and her parents. In spite of everything going on, he and Lila started having dinner together a couple of times a week and were slowly beginning to repair their marriage. He sensed a hesitation in Lila, but he didn't blame her, considering his own actions. He talked to his A.A. sponsor who said not to second-guess Lila and just concentrate on doing the right thing himself.

The twins were busy practicing reading. Pepper, the service dog, would be coming to school soon, and they were prepared. Lila was not sure how much reading and how much memorizing was involved, but their enthusiasm was contagious. Philip and Lila loved listening to them read and hearing them discuss their Halloween costumes.

Charlie wanted to be Pepper, and Charlotte had chosen a fairy princess costume, complete with wand, wings, and crown. There were no black Labrador costumes available, so Philip made a Labrador head out of papier-mâché and glued a black hood on the back to be worn over a black turtleneck. Charlie loved modeling it.

One evening at dinner, Philip asked Lila, "Will you ask Debo if I could go and see her sometime? I think she could help me spiritually, you know, since she is sort of a specialist in that field."

Lila could hardly mask her surprise. *Spiritual* was not a word in Philip's previous vocabulary. "I know she'd love to see you. I'm having lunch with her on Saturday. I'll ask her."

On Sunday, Philip went to the convent after lunch. Debo was waiting for him in the visitor's room. "So glad to see you, Philip!"

"Debo! You're just the nun I need to see!" They hugged briefly.

"Make yourself comfortable, and tell me what I can do for you."

Philip chose a straight-backed chair and sat on the edge. "As you know, I'm going to A.A.

and I sincerely want to stay sober, but I'm having a hard time getting a handle on God."

"I know what you mean. He's a slippery fellow. Our human minds can't get a hold of Him, but it is possible to have a trusting relationship with Him, and this requires very little from you."

"I'm not sure what you mean by a relationship with someone I cannot see or hear or touch. It doesn't make sense to me yet."

"I'm glad you added that *yet*. You've got an open mind. And always remember, God's name isn't Philip!"

"Thank God his name isn't Philip! Look where that got me. Where do I start?"

"I suggest you start with prayer. I'll tell you what I told Lila."

"You talked to *Lila* about prayer?"

"Yes."

"I never knew she was interested."

"Ask her about it."

"Sorry. I didn't mean to interrupt. I was just surprised. Please go on."

"A good way to start is by getting on your knees and repeating a prayer you know by heart, aloud if possible. The poetry of the prayer calms the mind and helps the brain produce alpha waves. These are the waves produced by meditation, and good poetry has the rhythm of our body pulses."

"Go on."

"Then, think of something you are grateful for or someone you love. You may feel yourself soften when you do this. After that, tell God, just as you would your own human father, what it is that you need from Him. End your prayer by thanking Him for understanding you. Once you have done this for a couple of weeks, let me know how it's going."

"What should I look for?'

"Don't look for anything. Just do it, and tell me what happens. You may find you have unexpected results."

"Do you think this will help me succeed in staying sober?"

"I think you succeed in staying sober as you succeed in anything else. You listen to the experts and follow their advice. Just like when you learned to sail a boat or play tennis. It is simple, but not necessarily easy. But people do things that are hard everyday. You are just one among many. Hard isn't the same as impossible. There's an infinite distance between hard and impossible."

"Do you know anything about alcoholism, Debo?"

"Well, I drank heavily when I was at MIT, but it wasn't difficult for me to stop. As I understand it, alcoholism is a physical allergy to alcohol coupled with a craving for it. Is that right?"

"Yes, that's what they told me at Anderson. They called it a mental obsession."

"I drank too much for a couple of years. That's for sure."

"It's not the same. I drank alcoholically from early on. I remember having blackouts at boarding school. I thought everyone had them, but apparently, social drinkers don't."

"I could've used them. I shudder to think of some of the things I said and did."

"Yeah, me too, but blackouts are no joke. I gave Charlie a black eye because I kicked the chair he was standing on and can't even remember doing it. I never want to do something like that again. I guess I'm lucky I didn't have the kids with me in the car and kill them both. I don't want to be that person any more."

Debo looked at her old friend and smiled. "I know it takes courage to change, Philip. I had to make a lot of changes too. But God does His part. He'll help you with this since you're willing. He helped me. As you may remember, I wasn't a natural for convent life."

"No, you weren't. You surprised us all."

"Tell me about rehab."

"I ended up staying there for five weeks and learned a lot about getting sober. Now I'm learning to stay sober. My roommate for four of those weeks just died of an overdose. He was such a smart and funny guy. He would have made a great A.A. member. Why did that have to happen?"

"It happened because he took too many drugs, Philip. God doesn't override our free will. There *are* consequences for our actions."

"Where's his spirit now?"

"I don't know. Every religion and philosophy has an explanation, and each one could be right in part. But what I do know is that man cannot create or destroy energy, we can only transform it. So, to me, it is only logical that something happens when we exit the planet. I'm sure there are more dimensions than the four we live in."

"I thought we only had three."

"Time, illusion though it is, counts as one."

"And what about the official position of the Church?"

"To summarize 2,000 years of theology is difficult, but simply put, the Church teaches that our spirits, our energy, if you prefer, become one with the Father, through the Son, yet we retain our uniqueness. I believe this. I believe we're spiritual beings having a human experience."

"So we're all children of light in God's sight?"

"Well, no. I don't think He's blind. He sees the difference between Mother Teresa and Hitler. Something *is* required from us."

Philip nodded his head thoughtfully for a moment. "I think sobriety is required of me."

"I think so too, Philip, but many blessings will come with that."

"They already have, Debo. I'm going to try prayer even though I don't have any experience."

"You don't need any. You'll notice a difference within three weeks if you do it daily. I've never seen it fail. "

"Thanks for seeing me, Debo. I'll let you know what happens."

Debo saw Philip to the door and watched as he drove out the convent gates and merged into the slow-moving Sunday traffic.

CHAPTER

15

In late October, the heat slowly released its stranglehold on the city. The wall of humidity finally shattered. There was freshness and fragrance in the air again. The cadence of daily life quickened, colors appeared more vivid, sounds sharper.

On Sunday night, Robert Hardy called Philip and asked him to come to New York. Philip reserved a room at a small hotel on Sixty-Third Street between Madison and Park where he remembered staying with his parents when he was six. For the first time in a long while,

Philip felt a pang of longing for his parents and memories of that trip flashed in front of him, ice skating at Rockefeller Center, drinking hot chocolate at Serendipity, and seeing *Cats!* on Broadway. There had been no drinking on that trip, and he remembered feeling safe and secure crossing the wide avenues, holding on to a parent with each hand.

Asher, Clarke's headquarters were midtown, on Park Avenue between 49th and 50th, a fifteen-minute walk from his hotel. The day was crisp and cloudless. Walking quickly, allowing the energy of the city to propel him, Philip entered the lobby. Sounds of the city muted immediately. Getting out of the elevator on the nineteenth floor, he checked in with the receptionist. The meeting was scheduled at four o'clock; he was fifteen minutes early. Sitting on a chrome and tobacco-colored leather sofa, Philip flipped through a glossy business magazine, paying no attention to the articles, his mind on the upcoming meeting. Hardy had sounded friendly enough on the phone, but being called to New York by the senior partner was unusual.

At four, he climbed the interior staircase to Hardy's office on the floor above. Hardy stood and stretched over his desk to shake Philip's hand. "Philip, I want you to know the people at Anderson have supplied us with a copy of the receipt for your computer. Of course, this takes all suspicion off you."

"Have you found out who is responsible?"

"Ned Kirby is quite accomplished in computer sabotage. He did a good job making you seem like the only one who could have changed the document. He did everything right, but he hadn't counted on your computer being locked up. The receipt from Anderson allowed us to confront him."

At first, Philip couldn't reply. The news of Ned's betrayal just didn't sink in. "It's hard to believe that Kirby would try to frame me."

"Well, start believing it. We caught him red-handed."

"How'd you catch him?"

"Knowing the changes couldn't have come from your computer made it easy. But I must tell you, we all thought you had done it. Once I knew Kirby was trying to throw suspicion on you, it all made sense. He was the one who brought you in my office when you were drunk, the one who pointed out the 'errors' in the document."

"I'll tell you what. Going to Anderson was the best thing that could have ever happened to me. But Ned Kirby really surprises me."

"He was asked to resign, lost his temper, and threatened a wrongful termination suit. Nothing will come of that though. He doesn't have a leg to stand on."

"I can't believe he did this."

"When a man shows me who he is, I believe him. Anyway, we're glad to have you back and hope you'll stay for the annual meeting. It starts with dinner at the University Club tomorrow night."

"Thank you. I look forward to that."

"Why don't you have dinner with me tonight, Philip? There are a few more things I would like to talk to you about, but I have a meeting now." Hardy stood. "Eight o'clock at the Harvard Club."

Philip left the office stunned and headed up Park Avenue toward his hotel. He couldn't get over that having his computer impounded had saved his career. It would have been believable, even to himself, that he was capable of making those currency changes in a blackout. And Ned. His good old buddy Ned. Philip's head was spinning.

Without thinking, he turned into the church on 60th and Park and sat in the back pew. The church was empty. Remembering Debo's directions for prayer, he got on his knees and stumbled through the Creed he had memorized at age twelve. He said it a second time with more confidence, thought of the twins and Lila, and thanked God that he was sober now and had not made the changes on the closing document. He didn't know what to think about Ned and decided not to think about him at all in this sacred space.

Once back at the hotel, Philip called Clay, his A.A. sponsor, and told him about Ned's betrayal, his indignation and anger increasing as the story unfolded. "That bastard tried to frame me."

Clay said, "Wait a minute. You're not a complete victim here. Can you see your part in this?"

"You mean because drinking made me easy prey?"

"Well."

"But this is a serious offence!"

"Don't get me wrong. I'm not defending him."

"Clay, this could've cost me my career."

"But if you hold on to rage like this, it's like slugging down poison yourself and hoping that bastard Ned will keel over."

Philip paused to let this sink in. "So what do I do?"

"Change your thinking. Accept the situation as it is, and acknowledge your part in it. Drop the charges in your mind against this Ned guy and become responsible for your own behavior."

"Well, this is a fairly unusual way to look at it. But I'll think about it while I'm here. I'm staying on for the annual meeting. Back Friday. Can you let me know where and when the A.A. meetings are here?"

"I'll call you in about an hour."

Philip then tried Lila's cell, but only got her voice mail and left a message saying that everything went really well at the office, that he had been invited to stay for the annual meeting, that he missed her and the twins and would be back on Friday. What he didn't say was that he was hurting. He had trusted Ned.

That night at the Harvard Club, Hardy told Philip that there was an opening in the Paris office starting in January, which would be a good fit for him. He told Philip to discuss this with Lila and give him a decision by November 1. Philip could go back to Tokyo and wrap things up there in November, be back in New Orleans for Christmas, and leave for Paris in early January. The firm used a relocation agency in Paris, which would find them an apartment and smooth the transition. Feeling sure that Lila would love living in Paris, he dared to hope this would sway her decision to start a new life with him.

Philip already knew some of the men from the Paris office and got to see them later that week. Glad to be with his colleagues again, Philip found it easy to order soda water at cocktail hour and to pass on the wine at dinner. What was surprising was seeing how little these men actually drank and realizing no one noticed or cared whether he was drinking or not.

The morning Philip left for New York, Lila came across an advertisement for a furnished two-bedroom carriage house in the French Quarter. On a whim, she called the agent and went to see it, a charming place with a brick courtyard and a huge live oak tree dripping Spanish moss.

The king-sized bed in the master bedroom stopped her in her tracks, realizing if she let Philip back into her life, this would be their bed. Did she want to restore intimacy to her marriage? She stood at the door and stared at it, unable to move on. Sensing the agent was anxious to get on with the showing, she said firmly in an overly loud voice, "I'll take it, if I can have a short-term lease." The sound and force of her own voice startled her.

The house was, in fact, available for three-month rentals. Lila called Ricky Wheeler, asking him to look over the lease, and signed for three months with an option to renew. Lila decided to keep this as a surprise for Philip.

On Tuesday afternoon, her mother helped her pack up their few things, and she and the twins moved into the carriage house. Finding a secret hiding place under the outside staircase, the twins played Go Fish while Lila unpacked. Lila loved the large, high-ceilinged main room and even the tiny old-fashioned kitchen. She thought how pleased Philip would be when he returned on Friday. She was missing him as were the twins.

On the flight back to New Orleans, Philip decided to present the Paris offer to Lila and trust God to guide her. Until now, he had never left any major decision up to Lila nor had he ever counted on God for anything, but he was confident this was the way to go. He had been praying for only six days, but he could already see changes in himself.

Lila and the twins met Philip at the airport, full of excitement. The plane arrived in time for an early dinner, and they went directly from the airport to The Bistro, a little restaurant two blocks from the new house. The twins were told not to tell Daddy anything about the house. They promised to keep this exciting secret but were bursting with the weight of their own responsibility.

Lila brought out coloring books and crayons to keep the twins happy, and Philip outlined the Paris offer. She burst into tears. Two anxious little faces looked up at her.

"Don't cry, Mommy. I'll look after you." Charlie had climbed down from his chair and went to his mother's side.

Charlotte turned to Philip and said, "Mommy's crying because she misses living with her parents. Tell her it's okay. They can come too."

It was Philip's turn to be confused. "Kids, don't worry. I think she's crying because she's happy."

"I am happy, and do we have a surprise for you, Philip!" Lila told Philip about her decision to put the family back together.

After dinner, they went to the new house. While showing Philip their room, the twins donned their Halloween costumes. Lila cranked up the music, and they celebrated, dancing in the courtyard by the light of the moon.

Later, Philip and Lila sat side by side in front of the fire in the living room. Philip took her hand and squeezed it hard. The familiar feel of his hand and the sight of their laughing twins gave Lila that grateful feeling in her upper chest. She smiled, recognizing it.

CHAPTER

16

Philip called Robert Hardy and accepted the position in Paris and packed his suitcase to go back to Japan. He called his A.A. sponsor and made appointments to Skype him twice a week from Tokyo. It wasn't easy with the time change, but Philip wanted to take good care of his sobriety. It was clear to him that if he lost it, he would lose everything.

After a tearful good-bye at the airport, Lila and the twins got *One Hundred and One Dalmatians* to watch that night and went to Paul's for a Sno-ball. Philip would be home in six weeks, and though that seemed like an eternity, Lila knew the time would fly. Her only worry was that Philip would be alone in Tokyo where he had easy access to his old habits. Debo reminded her there was something she could do about this.

Lila agreed to go to the Al-Anon meeting with Ricky Wheeler that Wednesday evening. The people attending the meeting were an interesting mix, a cross section of the city. What they talked about was similar to her experience, and she could relate to their feelings. It was odd to feel at home with a group of total strangers, and hearing the miraculous transformations that had taken place in their lives made her aware of how God was working in her own life.

Philip settled back into his life in Tokyo, but the drinking question weighed heavily on his mind. Skyping Clay the first time, he brought up the issue of business drinking in Japan.

"Clay, I never noticed what hard drinkers the Japanese are. I'm worried because there's a dinner being given in my honor by my biggest client. We drank a lot together, and I'm sure he'll expect me to match him sake for sake, and it'll be a twelve-course dinner."

"This isn't an unusual situation in early sobriety, Philip. There're old friends and business acquaintances that won't understand that you now choose not to drink. Though I do not ever recommend lying, this is the one exception to the rule. Two things you could say. Tell him that you've developed diabetes, and because of that, you can no longer drink. Be sure you pass on dessert as well, if you tell him this. Or if you think he is the kind of man who will still insist that you join in the toasts despite having diabetes, then tell him you have an allergy so strong that you can't breathe if alcohol gets into your blood stream. You can say this allergy runs in your family and that you had thought you had escaped it until recently. I've never known a person insist after hearing this."

"I'm going to go with the anaphylaxis reaction. No one wants ambulances or death at their dinner parties."

"This excuse has saved many difficult situations. And it's true, drinking is a matter of life and death for you."

"That's a load off my mind. I didn't want to tell him that I'm an alcoholic. He'd never understand."

"You never have to tell anyone you don't want to, except be sure to tell all doctors. This is important so that you are not put on any addictive medications."

"I'll let you know how it goes. Skype you later this week. Bye, Clay."

Even though the Williams' apartment in Tokyo was rented furnished, there was still five years worth of accumulation to be sorted out. Philip went through all of this, packing what would be needed in Paris, making piles of things to give away. While doing this he came across a box of baby pictures of the twins. His heart twisted at this evidence that he was barely present in their lives. Moving through the apartment while thinking of his resolve to change, he came to the bar. He stood up straight and surveyed the inventory. There were seventeen bottles. Without thinking twice, he called his neighbor, another American working in Tokyo. This man was sorry to hear the Williams family was moving, but glad to come and rescue the booze.

After the neighbor left, Philip sat on the living room sofa. The time was not right for calling or Skyping the States. This was the first time he had wanted a drink since he'd left Anderson. Fortunately, he'd been going to the English-speaking meetings in Tokyo on a regular basis and had the phone numbers of several men, which Clay had suggested he get just in case. Well, in this case, he needed someone else's strength to get to the other side of this craving. Calling the first man on the short list, Philip found someone who had first-hand knowledge of relapse. He shared his experience, and as Philip listened, his desire to drink died.

Philip missed Lila. He suddenly realized he had never before had this feeling of emptiness. He pictured Lila and the twins there at the carriage house and began, literally, to count the days until he would be with them again. He wanted to make up for his times of emotional and physical absence. He wanted to heal them with the force of his love. Would he be able to do this? He didn't know, but it was his primary aim.

The Reeves always celebrated Thanksgiving with a traditional luncheon. This year, they included all of the Parkers, Lila, her parents, and her younger sister Augusta, who was coming in from San Francisco where she was a partner in an eco-friendly textile design company. Angie, her Aunt May, and Sam Sanders were coming as well as Debo, Bobby, Ricky Wheeler, and several of the Reeve relatives and friends. They would be thirty in all, not including Samson and Delilah.

The large table was set with twenty-four places, six at the small one. Both tables had pale green damask tablecloths with matching napkins, large enough to be blankets for the twins. Mrs. Reeve had written the place cards in orange ink and did the seating with great care. Pumpkins and masses of gourds, interspersed with cabbages, pomegranates, and short crystal bud vases holding huge orange and dark pink lilies adorned both tables, along with the ornate family silver and pale green Venetian wine and water glasses. This was the first time the twins had ever had been included in a sit-down luncheon. Charlotte whispered that she thought fairies must have set the tables.

There was a lot of laughter at the small table where Lila was seated with the twins, Debo, Angie, and Sam. Sam was full of funny stories for the children and seemed at ease in their company. Angie was watching all of this from the other side of the table, imagining what a good father he would make. Lila and Debo were watching Angie watch Sam.

At the big table, another romance was burgeoning. Lila's sister, Augusta, was regaling Bobby with stories about her projects at Re Design, the company where she worked as a designer.

"Take these shoes for example." Augusta pushed her chair back slightly and angled her leg out so Bobby could see her red platform heels. "Fabulous for recycled PVC, aren't they?"

"Fabulous, as you say," Bobby said, admiring her long legs. "Do you design shoes for men?"

"In the works. But I do design wallpaper made from tires. So if you have any old tires, just send them on to me."

"What else can I send on to you?"

"Oh, your bamboo and your pineapples."

"And what will you do with my bamboo and my pineapples?"

"I'll make you a blazer or some curtains or something." Thinking how sexy it would be to get to know this Bobby.

"And where do you sell these masterpieces?"

"Trade shows only, so far."

"You know, every Christmas, I have a party for clients and friends at my art gallery. It's not a commercial thing, but I do like to have some sort of theme. Would your company be interested in shipping some samples? I could exhibit them for three weeks." This offer was not as altruistic as it sounded. Bobby knew from experience that all major sales were made before mid-December and that sales were flat until mid-January.

"I think I can speak for my partners, and we would love to send you our recycled debris for your Christmas party. But we want that trash back before the first of February."

"You're on."

All of this happened before the pumpkin pies came to the table. Coffee was served in the library, and Judge Reeve suggested that those who would like to could meet later at Preservation Hall to hear some jazz. Both Augusta and Bobby were enthusiastic about this.

It was late afternoon, and Lila announced that she should be taking the children home. They were getting tired. Augusta made a point of going home with them. She wanted to quiz Lila about Bobby. After putting the twins down for a nap, they went to the kitchen, and Lila grabbed the orange bag of Community Coffee. She slammed the cabinet door and flung the coffee on the counter.

Augusta did not seem to notice that Lila was out of sorts. She walked around the little kitchen, hugging herself with happiness. "Bobby said he would pick me up tonight. He is such an interesting man! How did I ever miss him?"

"Well, for one thing, he's nine years older than you are, Augusta. He'd already graduated from college when you were in the ninth grade. For another, he's a champion tennis player, and you've never batted a ball once since Mother and Daddy sent you to tennis camp. You would've seen plenty of him if you'd ever bothered to go to the Tennis Club."

Lila was surprised at the intensity of her own emotion. She managed to identify it as jealousy and was angry with herself for having it and angry with Augusta and Bobby too, but didn't know why. After all, she had made her decision to stay with Philip. Knowing it was irrational did not make the feeling go away. She breathed deeply, poured the coffee into mugs, and added scorched milk.

"Well, I can always take up tennis again."

"Not so easy, at your age."

"Lila! I am only twenty-five! And I get the feeling that I should move home and water my roots. Even if that means taking up tennis again."

"I thought you were sold on San Francisco. I thought you'd never move back here."

"I can do my design work anywhere. My partners don't need me to be in California. And I haven't had a real date in over a year. Let's see what happens with Bobby."

"Bobby Reeve has quite a reputation as a ladies' man. Proceed with caution and consider yourself warned."

"I'll keep that in mind. But he seems really nice to me. Anyway, I have to go. I have to change."

Lila wondered why she felt jealous. She called a woman she had met at Al-Anon and told her about the feelings she was having.

The woman surprised Lila by saying, "Good for you for identifying it. Go ahead and feel that jealousy. When it passes, you can think about it, consider your options, and decide what you want to do. I had a similar situation. And all I can tell you is that, for me, I made the right decision to keep my family together. Call me on Monday and tell me what you think after you've slept on it for a couple of nights." Lila thanked the woman and promised to call.

While Lila was sorting out her emotions, Augusta went back to her parents', put on a different pair of PVC shoes, jeans, and a pineapple fiber jacket. She looked a lot like Lila with long blond hair and blue green eyes, but she did not have the mind-set of a journalist, totally right-brained and thinking in terms of color and shape, and her administrative skills were limited.

Bobby was the first to notice that all eyes were on Augusta when she entered Preservation Hall and took a seat on one of the low wooden benches. Augusta seemed totally unaware of this attention, which was a big plus. Bobby thought he knew a lot about jazz, but Augusta knew more and her enthusiasm for the music and the band was contagious. It gave the night magic.

How did I ever miss Augusta? Is she too young to be interested in me? I have to be very careful with this one. Don't want to scare her off.

Bobby and Augusta made plans to meet at his gallery the following morning to talk about the exhibition, followed by coffee and doughnuts at the French Market. They wandered around the Quarter, inspected the artwork in Pirate's Alley, and sat on a bench in Jackson Square chatting until evening fell.

On the pretext of planning the exhibition, they saw each other all day Saturday as well, and Bobby took Augusta to the airport on Sunday. She promised to send the samples right away and return to help with the installation mid-December.

Bobby e-mailed or called Augusta nearly every day from then on. On the surface, it was all business, but they both knew something else was simmering behind this facade. *Bobby might be older by nine years*, Augusta thought, *but so what?*

CHAPTER

17

That Monday after Thanksgiving, Lila called her friend from Al-Anon and told her she had worked through her jealousy.

"Well, what road do you want to follow?"

"I want to stay with my husband. I don't know what I was thinking. I don't even really know Bobby. It was just a childhood fantasy."

"Is making this decision freeing for you?"

"I'll tell you what. I've really thought about it and know I want with all my heart to keep my family together. No one could take Philip's place in our lives."

"Sometimes, it's hard to leave dreams behind, but you've made a wise decision for yourself and for your children. Remember, you can always call me if anything else comes up."

Lila got right back into the routine of prayer and walks along the Levee while the twins were at kindergarten. And the three of them started preparing the house for Christmas. They wanted to have it ready for Philip's return.

Even with the time change between New Orleans and Tokyo, they did talk to or Skype Philip often, and Lila scanned their drawings and e-mailed them to Philip so that he could be a part of the Christmas spirit building in the carriage house.

Philip had been Skyping his sponsor in New Orleans regularly. There had been several situations he didn't know how to handle, but Clay's wisdom and practical suggestions had helped him through. He had gotten through the business dinner given in his honor without losing face and had gotten through the urge to drink. He had gotten through the packing and complicated leave-taking etiquette expected in Japan and arrived in New Orleans on December 15, just two days before the Christmas Pageant at Trinity Church. The twins only concern was that Philip would not recognize them in their costumes. Finally, Lila had to promise that she would point them out to their father before they could relax and go to sleep.

Augusta arrived two days later on the red-eye from San Francisco. Bobby was at the airport to meet her so that they could go straight to his gallery and work on the installation of the exhibit. With Bobby's party the next event on New Orleans's Christmas calendar, they had to work fast.

"So how do you think the eggnog will go with the organic bamboo wall hangings?" Bobby asked.

"I'm not so sure, but I wish I had thought of PVC mugs to drink it out of."

"Please, Augusta, I serve the really good eggnog. It merits fresh plastic."

"You'll never clean up the planet with fresh plastic, Bobby."

"Can we settle on washable, reusable, old-fashioned glass?"

"I totally approve. I'm going to make a mobile out of these shoes. What do you think?"

"I think you're beautiful."

"Keep working, Bobby."

At lunchtime, they walked over to Galatoire's where they found they knew many of the patrons and spent as much time greeting their friends and acquaintances as they did eating. Their being together was duly noted by all and would be reported citywide by evening.

On Christmas morning, after opening the stockings, the twins helped Philip make pancakes and bacon for breakfast while Lila supervised. She was aware that this was one of the happiest moments of her life. Feeling that sensation of gratitude in her chest again, she silently thanked God for all the decisions in her life that brought her to this moment. What a vast difference this Christmas was to the last one in Tokyo when the tension between them had been unbearable. She remembered spending the afternoon alone with the twins while Philip went to work. Today, she was looking forward to going to church and sharing this happiness with her parents. Looking across the kitchen table at Philip hugging a twin in each arm, Lila poured orange juice into the glasses.

The Christmas festivities passed in a whirl. New Year's Eve found Lila and Philip home with the twins, toasting marshmallows over the fire. Sam and Angie popped by unexpectedly, wreathed in smiles. They announced their engagement and promised the twins to make a stop in Paris on their honeymoon.

CHAPTER

18

Philip, Lila, and the twins arrived in Paris early on the morning of January 4. The city was still sleepy, and the great open sky was streaked with pale blue and grey, promising at least a glimpse of the sun that day. Their taxi stopped at a building designed by Baron Haussmann in the 1860s on the rue du Boccador in the 8th arrondissement. The concierge was waiting for them at the entrance of the building. She helped Philip take the bags into the interior vestibule and made sure the door to the street was locked. The tiny elevator would only hold two adults and the twins, without the luggage. Lila went up to the fifth floor with her and the twins.

Unlocking the door with a heavy iron key, the concierge showed Lila into the apartment. The real tour was different from the virtual one, and the length of the balcony surprised her with its ten large pots of dormant roses and solitary metal chair. Lila opened the doors to let in the morning air, and the twins, still in their overcoats, rushed out to play tag.

The décor of the apartment was a curious mix of inexpensive mass-market modern and classical French. The delicate winter sun was peeking into the apartment by the time Philip got the luggage into the rooms. They unpacked haphazardly and fell into bed for a nap.

The events of the last few months had convinced them not to spend any more of their Sundays in pajamas. Wanting their children to know the God they had waited so long to acknowledge, they signed the twins up for Sunday school at the nearby American Cathedral and made the commitment to go as a family.

Soon realizing that her schoolgirl French was inadequate to handle day-to-day needs, Lila found a teacher willing to meet with her at different cafes twice a week. This way, she got to know Paris and improve her French while the twins attended an international play school.

Business at Asher, Clarke was conducted in English, so Philip didn't notice how bad his French was until the weekends. He also noticed, or thought he noticed, that his colleagues were watching him carefully to see if he were drinking or not.

He Skyped his sponsor at 7:00 p.m., Paris time, on Tuesdays and Fridays. One Friday, toward the end of January, he brought up this subject. "Clay, maybe I'm being paranoid, but I think everyone in my office is watching me to see if I'm drinking."

"Well, your job requires discretion, and it's possible that one or two of the senior people in your office have been told to keep an eye on you, but I doubt if it's general knowledge."

"It sure feels like all eyes are on me when we're in a restaurant, like everyone's just waiting for me to drink the wine."

"Wine is part of their culture, and maybe they just want to make sure you have what you like.

Anyway, what they think is none of your business. Just make sure you're careful."

"I'm careful. Always careful. There's wine everywhere here."

"Why don't you talk to one of the men you know in A.A. there and see how they deal with it."

"I'll do that tomorrow. I'm making coffee for the Saturday afternoon meeting. There're several Americans and Brits there. I can ask one of them."

"Let me know what they say. I'd be interested. How are things, otherwise?"

"Otherwise, everything's great. Lila loves living here, and the twins have settled in. And I've gotten to the 8:00 a.m. English-speaking meeting every day this week."

"Good, and I'm glad you're doing the coffee on Saturdays. It's important to have a commitment to get you to the meeting on time and get to know the group."

"I like doing it. Have a good weekend, Clay, and I'll Skype you on Tuesday."

On Tuesday, the conversation continued. "I had coffee with an Irish guy after the meeting on Saturday. He's a photographer and has been living here for eight years. He's been sober for five and had some great advice for me."

"What'd he say?"

"He said the French are crazy about their livers. When he quit drinking, all he said to people was that he was *mal au foie*, that his liver was exhausted, and no one bothered him about wine ever again. He also said that the French are so polite that they do look to see if you have everything you want. So, I guess, I was just being paranoid."

"I'm glad you talked to him. Do you think he would be a good sponsor for you while you are there?"

"You're not firing me, are you?"

"Of course not. I just think you need someone in Paris to work with. I'll always be here for you, but face-to-face meetings are important for your success."

"You're probably right, but I'm astonished that I haven't had a desire to drink once since we arrived."

"Keep yourself connected, Philip."

CHAPTER

19

Augusta was still living in San Francisco, but things with Bobby had taken a personal turn. Bobby planned on going to an art fair there, but it was not scheduled until May, and he wanted a reason for seeing Augusta before then. On the spur of the moment, he decided to return the samples from the exhibition himself, hired a van, and started the cross-country drive in mid-January.

By the time he got to the Arizona border, he began to wonder why he had left his comfortable life to make this twenty-two hundred mile drive.

I must be crazy, he thought as he was pulled over for speeding. *I must be crazy*, he thought as he pulled into an uncomfortable motel for the third night. When he finally drew up to Re Design headquarters, he thought, *Whatever possessed me to do this?* His first glimpse of Augusta reminded him. They met at the bottom of the steps of the main entrance, where she was standing, waiting for him under an umbrella.

After they had unloaded the samples, they set off for Augusta's house on Walnut Street, which she shared with two friends from Stanford days. They took trays into the living room, lit the fire, snuggled up on the sofa, ignored the food, and got to know each other better.

While Augusta was working, Bobby haunted the art galleries, looking forward to their evenings together.

Then when Bobby was due to fly back to New Orleans, Augusta followed him to return the van. As she was driving him to the airport, she said, "I hate missing people, Bobby, and I know I am going to miss you."

"Why don't you move back to New Orleans? You can design there. Get an apartment in the Quarter. You would love it. I would love it."

"What about my two roommates who count on me for my part of the rent? Not to mention my business partners, who expect me in the office."

"Promise me you'll at least think about it."

"Promise." Augusta pulled up in front of Delta Airlines. Bobby kissed her sadly, grabbed his bag, and headed into the terminal building.

On Valentine's Day, a bouquet of fifty red American Beauty roses arrived for Augusta with a note. "One of us has to move. I love you. Bobby."

In early March, Ned Kirby called the Asher, Clarke office in New York and made an appointment to see Robert Hardy. He needed to somehow cajole a reference from this man. The last few months had been tougher than he expected, and getting a job with another firm with no explanation of why he left Asher, Clarke was no easy matter. Even though he still had plenty of money, he saw this would not last forever, and as a last ditch effort, he even contacted one of his law school professors for a character reference. The man never called him back. Now, he realized Hardy was his only hope.

Ned waited anxiously in the reception area for half an hour before he was finally shown into Hardy's office. Hardy was seated behind his massive mahogany desk, and Ned could tell from his face that this was going to be difficult. Ned began, trying to keep his voice jovial, "Mr. Hardy, you will be glad to hear that I'm not going to pursue my case against Asher, Clarke. But I would like you to write a reference for me."

"Ned, I can't do that. It's a serious matter to tamper with a closing document and frame a partner. In other circumstances, I might think about it, but these are exceptional."

"But, sir, I did this for the sake of the firm."

"Yes? In what way?"

"Well, Philip Williams was a wreck. His work was getting worse and worse. What could I do? That's why I maneuvered him into your office so you could see for yourself."

"Thank you, Ned," Hardy said dryly.

"It's not easy working with a drunk. I got sick of covering for him. I was just waiting for the big mistake. I knew he'd drag me down with him."

"There have been plenty of contracts drafted by drunks, even at Asher, Clarke. And it's our job to cover for each other. Not up to you to frame him. And you betrayed your oath as a lawyer."

Ned said nothing. Unable to remember his oath, he could only vaguely recall the ceremony when he was called to the bar. To him, this was a ceremony to glorify his right to make money. "I never planned on the client seeing that document."

"Do you remember what you swore?"

"What about the five years of sterling service I gave to the firm?"

"You were well paid for your services, Ned. I'm afraid there is nothing more I can do for you."

Ned left in a rage. Walking in the thin spring rain, hunched down in his trench coat, he hardly noticed where his feet were taking him. The rain had stopped by the time he found himself on the East River, near the Brooklyn Bridge. He scowled at the cold, muddy water. Never in his life had he not gotten his way, and he was determined

to get it now. After half an hour, he straightened his back and turned away from the river.
He remembered just the man who could help
him. This time, he would get it right. Get back
on his feet. Show the world what Ned Kirby was
really about. The ghost of a smile played on his
features as he walked briskly toward Chinatown.

Although she wasn't the kind of woman who
ever thought of money, Augusta hit upon a plan.
She would move back to New Orleans, take over
Philip and Lila's lease on the carriage house, and
save enough to pay off her credit card debt. It
was just a matter of persuading her partners at
Re Design that they could use a place in New
Orleans since so many trade shows were held
there, and the main room of the carriage house
was a perfect space for exhibiting their exciting
new designs. The rent seemed a bargain com-
pared to rents in San Francisco and Re Design
would pay it all.

As she walked into the house, empty since
Philip and Lila had left for Paris, she thought
she could detect Lila's rose perfume in the bed-

room. Standing at the window surveying the shady brick courtyard, Augusta wondered if roses could eke out enough sun through the oak leaves, hopeful that she could create a garden despite her black thumb. In the window boxes, which now held dead evergreen branches, she expected she could just about manage geraniums. Picturing them there, filling the space, round red heads erect above their frilly leaves, she decided she must have them. But only if they weren't expensive. Never again, she vowed, would she spend more than she made.

Moving in was easy since the place was furnished. Bobby came over most evenings after the gallery closed, and they often cooked together. Actually, Bobby was the better cook, but Augusta was gaining on him. They had been together for over three months, and by now, they were considered a couple. No one was more surprised and delighted by this than Mrs. Reeve. She had worried that the bachelor life suited Bobby too well. With Debo in the convent, he was her only hope for grandchildren.

Debo became a regular visitor to the carriage house, coming over most Saturday afternoons. Though Debo was crazy about Augusta's designs, her sense of color and proportion, what really fascinated her was raw material from the scrap heap being transformed into something functional as well as beautiful.

"You know, Augusta, what you are doing here is what God does with us humans."

"Well, Debo, I'll have to take your word on that. I wonder, do you have any advice on plants? I've got all these tiny geraniums. How big do they get? How many should I put in each box?"

Debo rolled up her sleeves. "Just leave this to me."

"But I want to learn."

"But look how you are dressed. Get me an apron, and you can watch."

Augusta returned with an apron and gloves. "I've got these."

"Never use them. I have to get my hands in the dirt to spread out their roots. Tricky business."

"When will they start to bloom?"

"When they're ready. Depends on the weather and how you treat them."

It was early May in Paris and the horse chestnuts were in full bloom. The huge panicles of pink and cream petals reminded Lila of the cherry blossoms she had loved so much during her years in Japan. But there is no place as beautiful as Paris, she decided. The twins were happy at play school and already had friends in the building, and Philip, well, she was falling in love all over again. And what a town for falling in love.

It all felt so different from when she left Tokyo. *How fast things can change*, she thought, remembering the dark days of Philip's drinking. Instead of expecting the worst, every day dreading his return from work, now they all looked forward to having him home. She wondered about prayer. What part had it played?

Philip liked his work. Once or twice a month, he was invited to join his colleagues for a drink at the end of the day in the neighborhood café. Some ordered wine and others ordered coffee.

Sam and Angie's wedding date was set for June 8, with Pastor Jim presiding at New Hope Baptist Church. Lila promised to fly back to

New Orleans to be matron of honor, but she would be coming alone since Philip was needed in his office and she did not want to disrupt the twin's schedule. Looking forward to spending some time with Debo, she planned to stay for five days.

By the time she left for New Orleans on the sixth of June, she knew the family would be fine without her. The day after she arrived, the rehearsal was at New Hope, followed by a dinner at Chez Hélène. Lila counted sixteen members of Sam's family who had come from Clinton, and Aunt May knew them all, although she had not seen them for years. Some had grown and some had shrunk since she'd last seen them. "My, how the years fly by," she kept saying. A few NOPD friends of Sam's and some of Angie's favorites from the hospital were there too. Forty-one people in all, ranging from age six to ninety. Debo was unable to join them since it was graduation time for her students, but Bobby and Augusta came hand in hand.

"So when are you two going to tie the knot?" asked Sam.

Augusta seemed flustered by the question, but Bobby answered smoothly, "Sam, I'll tell you what. You'll be the first to know."

The wedding was at four o'clock. Angie was gorgeous in her mother's wedding dress that she had dyed a delicate pale peach. Lila and the other bridesmaids wore lavender with matching organza picture hats. As she walked down the aisle on Aunt May's arm, a gasp went round the church. Many of the guests had only seen Angie in her choir robe or lab coat, and now here she was, bursting with beauty, about to marry.

Aunt May had decorated Angie's house for the reception with lavender roses, lilacs, and peonies and prepared the food with the help of three of her friends. The buffet table was crowed with jambalaya, crawfish etouffee, fried oysters, and other Creole specialties, a feast in the grandest Louisiana tradition.

Tapping her foot to the music, Lila watched the happy couple from across the room. Clutching her champagne glass, she thought about how she had almost lost her own marriage. What a good man she now had in Philip. She thought of the advice Pastor Jim had given her last September and looked around for him, hoping to have a chance to get him alone. Finding him on the porch, she pulled him to one side. "Thank you so much, Pastor, for the help you gave me last fall. I can't tell you how much I appreciated our conversation, and as you predicted, Philip's doing fine. I can't believe it, but I trust and respect him again."

"Yes, I remember well. He took the risk of opening his mind. Most addicts are so full of self-will that they just walk away from the light and continue down that dark hallway. Philip's one of the luck ones."

"Well, he has an A.A. sponsor here in New Orleans whom he talks to often. It's made a huge difference."

"True. A.A. has helped millions of people, but there're others who won't look at the harm they are causing. I suppose they're trapped. Remember, we talked about the prison of addiction."

"I remember. You know, Philip is the only person raised in Louisiana who can't make a decent cup of coffee, but they've got him making coffee for A.A. meetings in Paris these days. I started to tease him until I realized how much it means to him to be a part of making a meeting happen. There's a lot to be said for helping others."

"That's what life should be about, Lila. I'm so happy for you that Philip's on the mend."

"Have you met our friend Debo? Here she is. Come and meet her."

Debo stepped daintily down onto the porch. She looked surprisingly elegant in her simple dress, her face as lovely as ever.

"I've heard so many good things about you from Angie and Lila. I'm glad to finally meet you, Pastor."

"I'm honored, Debo."

"Well, since you two have much in common, I'll leave you together," said Lila, going back into the house to fill her champagne glass.

"Actually, I need a colleague to talk to. Between the ceremony and coming here, I had a call that a young man I've been counseling recently is back in jail. This boy is killing himself with alcohol and drugs and killing his mother with worry. Seems to me that some folks would rather be dead than change."

"Yes, the collateral damage is enormous."

"Right! When I mentioned to this boy how worried his mother was, he just shrugged it off, saying, 'That's her problem.' He has three younger brothers who need a role model too. Fine one he's setting. Not only causing harm, but missing a chance to be a force for good. It's a shame."

"I'll pray that he gets the gift of desperation."

"You think desperation is a gift?"

"Well, it's the raw material for radical change. Sounds like this young friend of yours needs that."

"Sure enough, he does."

After half an hour, Lila stepped back onto the porch to rescue her friend from what looked like a too serious conversation.

"Well, I believe I'll leave you two girls alone. I've certainly enjoyed meeting you, Debo, and seeing you again, Lila." Pastor Jim went back into the house to join the others.

"Lila," Debo said, touching Lila's arm. "Good news. I'll be taking my final vows in Rome on August 15th, and I've been invited to stay at our convent in Paris for the whole month of July. I talked to my mother this morning, and she and

Daddy would like to rent a house in Paris for that month. Do you have any suggestions on how to go about this?"

"The woman I found my apartment through is very good. I'll talk to her as soon as I get back. But this is great news!"

"Mother mentioned she would love to have your parents and Angie and Sam come to stay as well. So they'd like to rent a big house."

"A lot of families leave Paris in the summer. I bet she can find just the right place for them. I can't believe it, all of us in Paris together again."

"How do you like living there?"

"Philip's doing really well, and the twins have already picked up some French. I'm taking lessons twice a week and making slow progress, but it's all good fun. We love it. But, Debo, I've been meaning to ask you an important question. I've never really asked you since that first day when you didn't have time to explain about why you're becoming a nun."

"I promised I would tell you, but please keep this between the two of us. These things are personal and not easy to understand."

"Of course."

"It's hard to explain the call. It was a lot of little things. For instance, when I started going back to church when I was still at MIT, I was moved to tears during Mass. I know this doesn't sound like much, but I'd never been moved to tears before, and it got my attention. Then, I would have moments when I felt a sort of tugging at my heart when someone would tell me something personal. There were some other things too."

"Like what?"

"My grandfather died around the time I started going back to Mass. The morning he died, I was in my apartment, alone, and woke up at 5:00 a.m. with this great sense of joy. It was a laughing, dancing kind of joy, not a peaceful sort of joy. I felt this for hours. Daddy called me at ten to give me the news, and I couldn't take it in at first. He told me Papa had died of a heart attack at five that morning. I knew the joy I had that morning was Papa's joy.

"Then Daddy told me that Mother had woken up at that same time with a pain in her chest. He was about to call 911, when the pain stopped.

They decided to wait until nine and call her doctor, but the call came from Granny saying that Papa had died. Mother said her heart knew and broke. Later, she did see the doctor, and there was no evidence on the EKG of a heart attack. Strange, isn't it?"

"Yes, really strange."

"A few months later, I was coming out of Starbucks and looked up to see Papa waving at me. I saw him standing across the street in ordinary clothes, his brother next to him. They both looked young and happy. I don't know how I knew it was his brother since he'd died before I was born, but I knew. They were giving me a thumbs-up sign and laughing."

"But what made you think these were signs that you should become a nun?"

"There's more, but it did confirm my belief that our spirits are eternal. I've heard a lot of unusual stories from some very sane people. Like the experience you had under the skirted table at the time your grandmother died. And there's another incident, which occurred recently during one of my classes. Suddenly, the classroom started to shimmer, as if the dust motes had turned to glitter. I had an intense feeling that God's love for each one of my students was infinite and that his joy in them was that same dancing, laughing sort of joy I had on the day Papa died. I don't know how long this lasted. It felt like time had stopped. Anyway, I knew I was doing what he wants me to do. I have to do this, and I do it with joy."

"But you can be a teacher without being a nun."

"I know you might think being a nun is something small and dreary. But it's not. It's something vast and beautiful. I'm convinced that God can and does transform bruised and disordered lives, like mine, like Philip's, into something useful and whole. It's grace that does it."

"I know I should know what grace means, but I don't really."

"Grace is unmerited favor, Lila. And God is generous with that. You know, I was living a very self-indulgent life before, and now, well, I really want to become a nun. This is how I can serve God best. It's certainly not for everyone, but it's right for me."

"Debo, I'm privileged to have you as my friend. I cherish what you say."

"And, Lila, I feel sure that you are doing God's will for you too. Being a mother, wife, and journalist is a great blessing to many. But come on, enough of this serious stuff. Let's go join the party."

CHAPTER

20

The day Lila got back to Paris, she called the real estate broker to find a place for Debo's parents to rent, as she had promised. The best was a large house in Neuilly-sur-Seine, complete with cook and butler.

Sam and Angie, who would be spending a delayed honeymoon on Spain's Costa Brava, accepted the Reeve's invitation to end up in Paris. The Parkers, anxious to see the twins, were also delighted to get the invitation. The place in Neuilly would be a welcome change from the budget hotels they usually frequented. And

Bobby convinced Augusta to stop designing for a couple of weeks and start packing for Paris.

One night at supper, soon after her return from New Orleans, Lila turned to Philip and asked, "Whatever happened to that guy who busted you in Tokyo?"

"I've no idea, but I'll be talking to Robert Hardy tomorrow. As it turns out, I'm actually indebted to Ned Kirby, you know, Lila. If he hadn't pushed me into Hardy's office when I was drunk, I might never have gotten sober. I can't imagine being the man I was. So many changes have taken place since September."

"True. Wonderful changes."

The next afternoon, Philip called Hardy, who was in the New York office, and after their business conversation was concluded, he asked, "Have you heard anything from Kirby and his suit against the firm?"

"Well, yes. He came here a few months ago looking for a reference. Of course, I refused."

"I should tell you, I'm not entirely ungrateful to the man. He played a part in getting me to rehab, and so did you, Mr. Hardy. Thank you for that. I know I'd never have recognized the problem on my own."

"You're a good guy, Philip, and I'm counting on you to stay sober and make a difference in this world."

"And Kirby, what's going to happen to him?"

"We all have our choices, Philip, and some of us make bad ones. And you, you've turned the page. I'm proud of you."

The real sense of having turned a page came to Philip two days later on his way home from work. An elegantly dressed Asian woman was hurrying past. Suddenly, he heard her voice cry out in English, "God! Help me!" He turned and saw the woman lying on the sidewalk, being dragged by the strap of her shoulder bag by two young men, a third was blocking the view of the assault from the street. By instinct, Philip rushed toward her, but by the time he got to her, the assailants had fled without managing to snatch her purse. Philip helped her up and gave her his handkerchief to staunch the bleeding from her chin. Her knees were bloody too, and she was shaking. He took her to a café and offered her a brandy, which she refused, but asked for coffee.

"How can I thank you, monsieur?"

"Don't thank me. I'm just glad you called out in English. I might not have noticed otherwise."

"Oh, I'm from the Philippines. English is natural for me, even though I have lived here for many years."

After walking her back to her apartment building, Philip continued on his way home, realizing that the man who had run to this woman's aid was indeed a new Philip. Six months before, he probably would not have noticed what was going on after a few after-work martinis. Now he felt he was part of the human community again, no longer an outsider abstaining from interaction. No more excuses, lies, or blaming. No more causing harm—now even preventing it. He felt happy to be part of the greater world, removed from that rapidly shrinking world of his own making.

⁂

The house in Neuilly-sur-Seine sat on a carpet of perfectly raked pebbles behind an iron gate. You could see a large formal garden behind it through the tall windows, flanking the front door. It was as perfect a place in Paris as the Reeves could have ever imagined.

Mrs. Reeve loved the way the morning sun was slanting in through the windows framed by heavy silk curtains that ruffled in the breeze. "How do the French do it?" she asked her husband over a breakfast of café au lait and fresh, crusty baguettes. "It's all so perfect without looking like anyone called in a decorator."

Outside the kitchen door was a herb garden planted in a geometric design. Mrs. Reeve insisted on sitting out there every afternoon after a morning of museums. Bobby and Augusta set off for yet another round of galleries. Bobby's being in the art business meant Paris was heavy work for him, but Augusta found it all very glamorous.

Paris was also a special place for the Reeves. Mrs. Reeve had spent the summer when she was nineteen living with a French family on the boulevard de Beausejour in the 16th Arrondissement. That summer, she drank at least one of her many coffees per day at La Rotonde de la Muette and made it a destination on every subsequent trip to Paris. She loved the old-world glamour, wood paneling, red velvet banquettes, and shiny brass bar. She was delighted to find the same red lampshades casting romantic light all around, even onto the street outside. All this combined with great sixties blues made her feel nineteen again. Always a good feeling. Now, the chef was Moroccan, and they serve one of the best tagines in all of Paris. "Some things change, some things stay the same," Mrs. Reeve laughed as she tucked into her first tagine.

As for Judge Reeve, he had been treated to lunch at Le Grand Véfour by his grandfather when he was twenty-one. Older than the French Revolution, this restaurant is still located in the arcades of the Palais Royal and still retains its gilded and mirrored interior.

One day after a splendid lunch there, Bobby and Augusta went off for a walk while the Reeves headed home, Debo to the convent. They stood in front of the column in the Place Vendome admiring the architecture, then went into the Ritz bar, and over a glass of champagne, Bobby took Augusta's hand.

"Look, Augusta. I've been driving myself crazy thinking what to say to you, and I thought of just the right thing, but now I've forgotten it. The gist is: please marry me right away."

Augusta wrapped her long arms around Bobby's neck, almost spilling both glasses of champagne, and whispered, "Bobby Reeve, what took you so long to ask?"

Bobby paid the bill, and they strolled into the July afternoon. Just a few steps from the Ritz was Boucheron, where Augusta chose a nine-carat sapphire from Kashmir. Its solid blue mass suited Augusta perfectly, but it needed to be made one size smaller. The salesman said it could be resized in three days. Deciding to keep their engagement secret until the ring was ready, they left the store, arms around each other's shoulders. Augusta thought it was all like a dream or a movie. Getting engaged in Paris. Who would have ever thought life could be so perfect?

Sam and Angie were the next to arrive, followed by the Parkers the next day. Lila, Philip, and the twins joined everyone that night, picking Debo up at the convent on their way to the Reeves' house in Neuilly.

There was smoked salmon followed by Sole Vèronique and moelleux au chocolat. "Only the

French could take a basic brownie recipe and turn it into a gourmet dessert," Mrs. Reeve said.

Bobby gently tapped a spoon against his wine glass to call for silence and stood up. "Thank you all for being here tonight to share a very special occasion. Not only are we all in Paris together, but Augusta and I have an announcement. Three days ago, Augusta promised to be my wife."

For a brief moment, there was silence around the table. Then, laughter erupted with cries of congratulations. Bobby slipped the ring on Augusta's finger. A few tears slid down her smiling face as she hugged Bobby with one arm and reached for her mother with the other.

After the excitement had settled down, Debo tapped her glass. She stood and turned to Bobby. "Bobby, I want to congratulate you on your good sense and your perfect timing." She looked at Augusta. "And, Augusta, I'm thrilled to have you as my sister." She looked around at each of the guests. "Could any of us have dreamt of this night a year ago? Imagine the number of coincidences that took place to bring us all here." No one spoke as each one was trying to summon up faith in coincidence and coming up with nothing. "I would like to propose a toast to God whose fingerprints are visible on all of our lives."

"Yes," said Philip, standing up to join her. "And I would like to thank more than one person in this room, God included, not for a coincidence, but for a miracle. My sobriety. I could never have done this on my own."

"You didn't have to, Philip. God is generous every day."